M.H. NORRIS

PRO SE PRESS

PRO SE PRESS

BADGE CITY: NOTCHES
A Pro Se Press Publication

Edited by Greg Gick, James Bojaciuk, and Jason Norton
Editor in Chief, Pro Se Productions—Tommy Hancock
Submissions Editor—Barry Reese
Director of Corporate Operations—Morgan McKay
Publisher & Pro Se Productions, LLC Chief Executive Officer—Fuller Bumpers

Cover art and logo design by Jeffrey Hayes
Print production and book design by Forrest Dylan Bryant
E-book design by Russ Anderson
New Pulp logo design by Sean E. Ali
New Pulp seal design by Cari Reese

Pro Se Productions, LLC
133 1/2 Broad Street
Batesville, AR 72501
870-834-4022

editorinchief@prose-press.com
www.prose-press.com

BADGE CITY NOTCHES

CHAPTER ONE

Grace

CURLED UP UNDER a tree in the middle of Coal Hill Park, the girl lay in such a way that Detective Deidre Tordano could almost imagine that she was sleeping and dreaming of princesses and ponies, sunshine and rainbows

The camera flash could be mistaken for a parent taking a picture of her sleeping child, wanting to hold that memory for years to come.

The leaves crunched under Deidre's feet as she got out of her car.

"Got the call an hour ago, jogger found her on the trail. She was left with her backpack that had an ID in it. Grace Miller." Officer Hamilton walked up to her, clipboard in hand.

"How old?"

"Ten."

A gust of wind blew past them and Deidre pulled her trench coat closer. "Coroner's here?"

"Just arrived a few minutes ago. CSU is almost done with the scene."

Deidre nodded as she stepped up and ducked under the

tape. The body of the girl—of Grace—lay to her right, a pink jacket in a bundle to the side. But it was far too big to belong to the girl. "Did the jogger cover the body?"

"No, we believe the killer did that."

Deidre pulled out her notebook. "Remorse, maybe?"

The photographer lowered his camera after one last flash. "I'll have these on your desk in an hour."

"Thanks." Deidre walked up to the coroner, Angus Ramsey, who knelt beside the body, covering one of the girl's arms from sight.

Sliding on a pair of rubber gloves, she knelt down beside him, trying to catch what had him so interested. "Did you move that jacket and possibly contaminate my crime scene?"

"I didn't know this was 'tell me how to do my job' day."

"They got a picture, right?" She took in the sight of the young girl who lay on the ground before her. Blonde hair framed the young face and Deidre had to resist the urge to brush it away.

"Yes, I made sure. Now, take a look at this." Angus shifted so that Dedire could see the victim's arm. "Feel that."

"Do I have to?" Deidre ran her hand over a cut in the arm which was located just below the shoulder. "What am I supposed to be feeling?"

"That one is deep enough to hit the artery. The one right below it is, too. If your unsub started from the bottom and then finished here, your victim could have easily bled out."

"Then where's the blood?"

"That's your job to figure out."

"Don't remind me. Who would do this to a kid?"

She took the arm from Angus, running her fingers carefully over the remaining five cuts, the ones that weren't as deep. Setting it back down, she peeled open the girl's eyelids, revealing dull green eyes. "She's been dead for a couple hours at least. If our witness found her a half hour ago, she could have been lying here for at least an hour."

"I'll get to work on her autopsy. Should have the preliminary report for you first thing tomorrow."

"Thanks, Angus." Her phone started to ring and she walked away from the scene as she saw the screen light up with her husband's number.

"On your way, sweetheart?" her husband answered.

"I wish I was. Listen, I'm not going to make it."

"What's wrong?"

"Homicide. She was only ten. I've got to go tell the parents. I'll try to make it home in time for dinner, but I might have to pick something up."

"Don't worry about it. I'll get the kids and we'll make something work."

"Thanks."

"Love you."

"Love you." She tapped End Call. "Did someone run a check on the victim's family? Was there a missing persons report filed?"

"Not that we have." Officer Hamilton handed her his clipboard. Deidre skimmed the contents and didn't see anything that would raise red flags.

"Now about this book bag." She knelt beside it before unzipping it. Inside, she found a reader, a folder, and a crumpled up soccer uniform. "Where was she headed?"

Deidre rose as the coroner's assistants loaded the body into a bag before placing it on a gurney. "Anything from our witness?"

Officer Hamilton shook his head. "Officer Jacobs is taking her statement now, but from what I heard, she just found the body. Didn't even realize the girl was dead."

"Put her statement on my desk and I'll read it when I

get back." Deidre scanned the area. "The unsub must have carried the body and posed it. No drag marks."

"And since it's a public trail, processing footprints is almost impossible. And we haven't been able to find any usable fingerprints."

"Maybe something at the vic's home will shed some light." Glancing at the clipboard, she read the address and realized she had fifteen minutes to figure out how to tell Grace Miller's parents their little girl wasn't coming home.

Pulling to the road, she picked up her phone and dialed her partner's number, but received no answer. She dialed another familiar number. "Hey, I need a favor."

—

A SIMPLE WHITE two-story house met Deidre as she pulled up to the Miller home. Picket fence, flowers by the front steps, minivan with a soccer bumper sticker, plenty of touches that made it look like any other home. Nothing showed that their world was about to be turned upside down.

Parking her car, she tapped the steering wheel and let out a grunt of impatience as she waited.

"I'm sorry to inform you, Mr. And Mrs. Miller, I am sorry to inform you but… Grace is dead. Your daughter is dead. I'm sorry to tell you, but your daughter is dead."

How sad was it that she was going over ways to tell a family that their daughter was dead?

She slammed her hand against her steering wheel, taking care not to honk the horn. A child, a little girl, and someone had the audacity to…

Deidre knew she shouldn't let this bother her so much. She'd been doing this for far too long. But there was something about it being a kid this time. It made her think of the four she had waiting at home.

The sight of a familiar car turning onto the street pulled her out of her thoughts. She watched as the department chaplain pulled up, coming to a stop across the street.

Nodding to him, she got out of her car. "Thanks for coming so fast, Rick."

"Glad I could be here to help. Although I do say, I don't envy you right now. What do we have?"

Stopping before the front gate, she turned and lowered her voice. "We've got a 10-year-old girl and I have to tell her parents that they won't see her again."

"What happened?"

"We're not completely sure, but it looks like someone cut open her arm and let her bleed out."

"Any leads?"

"None. Though something tells me the notches on her arms mean something." That same something told her that she didn't want to find out what.

A gust of wind blew, causing both to shiver before Deidre nodded and turned to the gate. "Well, let's take care of this."

Opening the gate, she let Rick through. It shut with a loud, hollow, clank. Taking a deep breath, she made her way down the walk, towards the waiting door, hearing the footsteps of the chaplain behind her.

They didn't make it to the door before it opened, revealing a mother who kept one hand firmly on the jamb. "Can I help you?

"Mrs. Stephanie Miller?"

"Yes."

"I'm Detective Deidre Tordano and this is our precinct chaplain, Rick Ayers. May we come in?"

"What's wrong? Is it Jason? He was supposed to be picking up Grace…she spent the night at a friend's house and they were going to soccer practice together. He left his phone here and I've told him not to leave home without it…"

"Mrs. Miller, may we come in?"

"Of course."

Slowly the door opened, but Mrs. Miller's hand stayed firm on the edge as she held it open. "Are you alone?"

"For now. Jason went to pick up Grace. My oldest daughter, Leslie, is at the library working on a project and my other two children are at their grandparents."

"You said your husband left his phone here, but is there someone I can call?"

"Why, what's going on? What's wrong?"

"Have a seat, ma'am."

The front door burst open and a man came rushing in. "Stephanie, it's Grace!"

Mrs. Miller's eyes darted between the foyer and Deidre, and Deidre couldn't help but feel her stomach sink.

Finally, Mrs. Miller found her voice. "What about her?"

"She's missing. She wasn't at soccer practice and Nancy's family hasn't seen her since she was dropped off." Mr. Miller came into the living room, eyeing Deidre and Rick. "Who are you?"

Pulling out her badge, Deidre nodded to the couch where Mrs. Miller was sitting. "Detective Deidre Tordano. Take a seat, Mr. Miller."

"How can I take a seat?" Mr. Miller shouted. "My daughter is missing."

"Take a seat." Deidre pulled up a chair.

"What part of 'my daughter is missing' do you not understand?"

"You know where she is, don't you, Detective?" Mrs. Miller's question was quiet, hesitant.

"I'm sorry. I hate to be the one who has to tell you this, but…your daughter is dead."

"What?" Mrs. Miller started shaking as her hand went to her open mouth. "No, no, no, you're wrong."

"I'm sorry. I wish I was."

"What happened?" Mr. Miller scooted closer to his wife. "What happened to my baby?"

"We won't be sure until the autopsy is completed. But we think someone…"

"Someone what, Detective?" Mr. Miller's voice was low, anger filling it. "What did someone do to my daughter?"

Deidre looked at Rick, who nodded reassuringly at her.

Turning to the Millers, she leaned forward. "From what we could see at the scene it looks like someone cut open her arm, and let her bleed out."

There was no response, only silence.

"And where were you when this happened, Detective? Where were you when this sicko killed my baby girl?" Mr. Miller stood to his feet and got in Deidre's face. "Why didn't you stop it?"

"We didn't know."

"How could they know?" Mrs. Miller spoke up, her eyes filling with tears. "How could they know? We should have been there; we should have kept an eye on her. Oh my baby. My baby girl."

The couple embraced as Mrs. Miller started sobbing.

Deidre allowed them a minute. "Is there someone I could call? A pastor? A friend?"

"Reverend Allan Jacobs."

"Redeeming Grace Baptist?" Deidre pulled out her phone, Googling the church.

"That's the one."

Deidre excused herself and dialed the number. After a minute, a voice answered. "Thank you for calling Redeeming Grace, where we celebrate the redeeming grace of Christ. This is Reverend Jacobs."

"Reverend, this is Detective Deidre Tordano."

His voice lost the light tone as he answered. "What happened?"

"Grace Miller's body was found a couple hours ago."

A gasp could be heard through the line. "What happened?"

"Looks like someone cut her open with a knife."

"That poor girl."

"Can you come to the Millers' house on New Hampshire? They asked for you."

"Of course." She heard rustling on the other end. "I'll be there in a few minutes."

"Thank you."

Deidre hung up and headed back into the living room, pulling out her notebook. "I'm so sorry, but I need to ask you a few questions about Grace. You said she was at soccer practice?"

"Yes, she plays for the Red Wings at the Westlake Rec Center."

"So she was getting ready for the tournament? I know my daughter is."

Mrs. Miller nodded, grabbing a tissue. "She was so excited."

Deidre made a note, considering her next question. "Did she participate in any other activities?"

"No, just soccer. She did her homework, played with her dolls, and loved to write in her notebooks." Mrs. Miller grabbed another tissue.

"Have you seen her talking to any strangers the last few days?"

"No, she knows not to talk to strangers." Mr. Miller stood up and began pacing the room. "She's not gone. You're wrong. You must have mixed up the ID; something."

"Her backpack was with her. I'm sorry." Deidre picked up the folder from the table earlier and handed it to Mrs. Miller. "You'll find some resources, support groups, some things to help you get through the next few days. I'm sorry, but they're going to be hard because there are going to be officers in and out, asking questions, going through Grace's room; anything that can give us a clearer picture of what happened."

The next few minutes passed as Deidre answered their questions, but she just barely held in the sigh of relief when the doorbell rang. She got up to answer it and found Reverend Jacobs standing at the door.

"Thank you for coming."

"I'm assuming that they can't have the body until you are done with your investigation?" the Reverend asked.

"Right. If they want to do something the next few days, it will have to be just a memorial." Deidre stuck her head back into the living room, waving at Rick to follow. "I'm so sorry for your loss. My card is in the folder and I'll be in touch."

Leaving, she heard Rick behind her and turned to him. "If I never have to do that again, it will be too soon."

—

SOCCER PRACTICE WAS in full swing at Westlake Rec Center as Deidre pulled into the parking lot. Inside she found several people waiting for her. She quickly recognized one as the manager of the center, Alexandria "Lexi" Lestrade, standing with a man whose face was full of worry. She watched as Lexi ran a hand through her dark hair before tucking it behind her ear.

Lexi finally noticed her as she walked up to the pair. "Detective Tordano." Not for the first time, Deidre had to wonder why this young woman was running a rec center when she could have been out doing better things. But considering how much her daughter, Lilly, loved "Miss Lexi," she couldn't complain all that much.

Deidre turned to the man next to Lestrade. "Are you Grace Miller's coach?"

"Yes. Harry Slade." He held out his hand.

"Detective Tordano." She shook it before pulling out her notebook. When was the last time you saw Grace?"

"She had the early practice today, and it ended around 9:30, but her grandparents were running late. She said she was going to wait in here and work on homework."

"Would explain the backpack." Deidre continued writing. "Did you see her after she came in here?"

"I did," Lexi spoke up. "I came in after checking on the next practice to get some paperwork done and she was sitting over there."

Deidre walked in the direction that Lexi pointed before spotting something red on the table. "What the?"

There on the table was a red six carved into the side of the table and filled in with red… well–she hoped it was marker. But CSU might have to double check that.

"What?" Lexi came over. "Where did that come from?"

"You've never seen it before?"

Lexi shook her head. "No, I take great care to keep this rec center in good shape. The city won't replace anything, so what we've got is what we've got."

"What do you mean?"

"They want to shut this down. Say it will save money. But these kids need the leagues."

Deidre grabbed the gloves out of her jacket pocket and slid them on, running her hand over the six that was carved into the corner of the table. "What does this mean?"

"What carved that?"

"You didn't see anyone here?"

Lexi shrugged. "People come in and out of here all day, especially with practices."

Looking around the empty room, Deidre tried to start putting the pieces together. Pulling out her phone, she called Dispatch. "I need a CSU to Westlake Rec Center, ASAP."

"10-4."

Hanging up, she turned to Lexi. "I'm going to have to lock this down until they're done. If anyone has stuff in here, tell them they can come back later when I release the building."

"I'll make an announcement." Lexi turned to leave. "I can't believe someone did this to Grace."

"I'm going to figure out what happened to her. But I might be back with more questions."

"You know where to find me."

Deidre turned back to the table, then back to the room, then back to the table. What happened here?

CHAPTER TWO

Home

Deidre pulled into the garage, thankful her husband had left the overhead light on. The sun had set about an hour ago and she was no closer to even beginning to figure out what had happened to Grace Miller.

Picking up her laptop case, she grabbed her travel mug and pushed the button on the box that rested on her visor, shutting the garage door. She made her way to the back door, stopping just inside to deposit her gun belt into the safe before entering the kitchen.

Opening the mudroom door, she heard the sound of upbeat music and the lyrics of some catchy song she'd heard her two youngest, Colton and Carrie, sing on the way home from church. Walking in, she leaned against the doorway and watched as her husband, Bill, flipped pancakes out of the pan as the twins danced beside him. All three were swaying to the beat of the music and didn't notice her.

Carrie finally looked over and charged. "Mommy! We got our green belts today."

Deidre knelt down and gladly accepted her daughter's hug. "I know. I wish I could have been there."

"Were you out catching bad guys?" Colton came for a hug as well.

"Trying to." Deidre looked between the kids.

"Daddy said after dinner we could show you our new belts and act out our graduation for you."

Deidre looked up at her husband. "He did?"

Both nodded.

"I love the idea." Deidre pulled both into a hug. "Now I think Daddy's almost ready with dinner. How about you two go wash up."

They took off and a few seconds later she heard the pounding of footsteps on the stairs. Shaking her head, she turned to Bill. "Thanks for making dinner."

They exchanged a quick kiss. "We had fun."

Deidre looked at the white powder that settled on the counter. "I can see that. What surprises me is some of the mix made it into the pancakes."

He flipped one of the pancakes and smiled sweetly. "They wanted to help mix it. You okay?"

"I'll be fine." Deidre rubbed her temples, feeling a headache coming on.

"If you want to talk…"

"Maybe later."

"Okay. Want to go find Mac and Lilly?"

"Sure." Deidre left the kitchen and headed upstairs.

She knocked on Lilly's door and heard pop music playing on the other side. "Lilly, it's me. Can I come in?"

"Sure."

Opening the door, she noticed the unmade bed and shook her head, remembering her conversation with Mrs. Miller earlier. "How was your day?"

"Good. Can you look this over after dinner?"

Deidre glanced at the math sheet in front of her daughter

and held in her groan. “Sure thing. Want to head down and start setting the table?”

“Can I finish first?”

Deidre nodded, and Lilly turned back to her worksheet, humming away to Dreamer’s newest CD. Watching her for a minute, Deidre left the room and headed down the hall to another room where hard rock music blasted. Knocking, Deidre let out a knowing sigh. “Mac?”

The music continued to play and Deidre tried again before simply opening the door herself. Her oldest sat at his desk, drumming with his pencil instead of using it. Looking at his shaggy mop, Deidre realized that maybe he was due for a haircut. “Mac?”

“When did you get home?”

“A few minutes ago.”

“Dinner ready?” Mac went over to the stereo and paused it.

“Almost. How about you head down and help your sister set the table?”

With a sigh he got up. “Okay, mom.”

Deidre fell in step beside her son. Already Max was almost as tall as she was, and the growth spurt showed no signs of stopping. “How was school?”

“Okay. I’ve got to stay after tomorrow for auditions.”

“Let your dad know. Which musical is it this year?”

“*Into The Woods*.”

“Well, break a leg, kid.”

“Thanks, Mom. Hey, are we still going to the Children’s Museum this weekend for the Shakespeare exhibit?”

“I think that’s still the plan. Hopefully, I can step away long enough. Head down in a minute, okay?”

Deidre headed back downstairs and suddenly found two bundles clinging to her legs. Looking down she found the twins; their hands were washed but clothes were still covered in flour. And now, so were her pants.

"Hi, guys."

They followed her into the kitchen where Bill was finishing the cooking.

"Lilly! Mac! Get down here and set the table!"

"Coming!" Lilly's voice rang down.

Eventually, Lilly and Mac came down, the table was set and Deidre found herself sitting around it with her family.

Grace was said and food was passed.

"What's everyone have planned for tomorrow after church?" Deidre took a bite of the pancakes. Nothing quite like breakfast for dinner.

"I have a game. Can you make it?" asked Lilly.

"I'm not sure, sweetie, I'll try. Mac, you said you have auditions?"

Mac nodded.

"We're going with Grandma and Grandpa," Colton said with a mouthful of food.

"Don't talk with your mouth full."

Colton nodded before swallowing his food. "Sorry, Mom."

Deidre smiled, ruffling his hair. "It's okay, bud."

A few hours later, Deidre lay in bed and blissful silence met her until the bedroom door opened and closed and she felt someone crawl into bed next to her. "Long day?" her husband asked.

Deidre rolled over to face him. "I've seen a lot of things over the years, but this time it was a child. Who would do something like that?"

"You'll catch him."

"That doesn't help the Miller family." She turned back over.

"It helps them have closure."

Letting out a sigh, she shrugged. "Yeah."

"Get some sleep."

"Something tells me I'm going to need it."

CHAPTER THREE

Flip a Coin

Her alarm and cellphone went off at the same time and with a groan, Deidre hit the snooze button before picking up the phone. "Tordano."

"Heads or tails?"

Deidre sat up and looked at the caller ID and saw that it was Jackson. "It's six in the morning. I'm not flipping a coin with you until at least eight."

"We've got three scenes to look at."

"What are you talking about?"

"Ten-year-old Jessie Phillips went missing some time during the night from her bedroom over on Bragg Court. Her parents went to check on her this morning, only to find the room empty. It looks like whoever it was broke in through the window, but there is no sign of struggle."

"And what's behind door number two?" Deidre got out of bed, taking a second to turn off her alarm.

"Ten-year-old Emily Lee was also kidnapped from her home on Clarke Street sometime during the night. Once again, when her parents went in to check on her, the room was empty. Signs of damage to the window, no signs of struggle."

Deidre turned on the bathroom light and put her phone on speaker so she could brush her teeth. "And number three?"

"Jessie Phillips' body was found ten minutes ago by a janitor at the Children's Museum."

Taking a second to spit, Deidre turned off the water. "Notches in the right arm?"

"Just like Grace."

"We take the scene with the body first. Send a secondary team to the other two. Is an Amber Alert out on Emily?"

"Yes."

Deidre headed downstairs and started the coffeepot. "I'll meet you at the museum in a half hour."

Heading back upstairs, she made her way into the closet, taking care not to wake Bill. Dressing in the dark, she double-checked her appearance in the bathroom mirror. She'd learned the hard way a long time ago why the double-check was necessary. Rubbing her hands over her face, she grabbed a ponytail holder and claw clip and threw her auburn hair up nice and simple.

She stopped by each of her kids' rooms, peeking in to make sure that there were four sleeping figures.

Back downstairs, she breathed a sigh of relief when she found a full coffeepot. She grabbed the biggest travel mug they owned and filled it with the black liquid, cream and sugar.

And with that, she was gone.

—

SHE TURNED ONTO the road and could see the Children's Museum ahead. Lights flashed, the road was blocked, and cars honked repeatedly as they were redirected elsewhere. Turning on her lights, she forced herself through the jam to the barricade to find Rookie Officer Hale standing nearby.

"Drew the short straw this morning?"

He grunted as he moved the barricade aside to let her through. "You could say that."

"Thanks for putting up with it." Deidre raised her window and drove through, parking just outside the front doors of the museum. The normally cheerful and bustling building, now a quiet crime scene. The yellow crime scene tape crossed the entrance in a sad sort of way.

On the other side of the barricade, she could see a small crowd of people, along with news teams and both regular and video cameras. Something told her this was going to be a long day.

Taking a large sip of her coffee, Deidre got out and made her way up the stairs. She ducked under the tape, nodding thanks to the officer that held it. Signing into the log, she made her way inside. Downstairs, a crowd of policemen surrounded a room with glass walls. The officers parted, providing her with means to view inside.

Lying against the corner was another girl, this time in her PJs. Hair, while in cornrowed pigtails, showed signs that she had been sleeping before she'd been taken. A clear smock covered her as if she had been tucked in. If her location, or the fact that she was surrounded by the police hadn't given away that something was wrong, once again Deidre would simply have guessed the child had fallen asleep after having too much fun.

The glass walls were clean, ready for a new day. Inside the cube, cameras flashed as the CSU analysts photographed the scene. She knelt down next to the body and something in the corner caught her eye. It was a crude drawing of two stick figures with long hair, holding hands. Where their hands met, a red line curved up from the bottom to cross the smaller figure out.

"Someone's trying to say something." Deidre moved aside so the photographer could take a picture. "Has Angus been called?"

"He's on his way." Officer Hamilton walked up carrying his ubiquitous clipboard. "Body was found by a member of the custodial staff, about an hour ago. His statement is under the initial report."

"What about the security system?" Deidre nodded to a camera that was in a corner by the ceiling. "Did they pick anything up?"

"Whoever did this cut the wire. The camera is down."

"'Course he did. How did he even get in here?"

"We're still working on those details, but it looks like they temporarily cut power to the building and used the three minute reboot to get in and out. There's a team looking at the log of the outage last night."

"Who would know how to reset the system like that?" Flipping through the clipboard, Deidre turned as Angus walked in. "We need to stop meeting like this."

Angus let out a grunt. "Or wait for a more decent hour. What do we have?"

"Looks like our guy."

"Notches?"

"Haven't checked yet."

"Well." Angus slipped on a pair of gloves. "Shall we?"

Deidre followed him back inside the glass cube. Angus knelt beside the body, turning her flat. Sure enough, there were five notches on her arm.

"Again, these look deep enough to cut the artery."

"And again, no blood. What did Grace Miller look like?"

"Still working on my report, but she's missing a substantial amount. It's pretty safe to say that she died due to blood loss."

"Which means somewhere there's a crime scene with serious traces of blood from at least two corpses."

"Something else to note." Angus held up the arm.

"What's that?"

"All of these cuts are deep enough to knick the artery. With Grace Miller yesterday, that wasn't the case. There was hesitation cutting. Whoever did this is getting comfortable slicing up people, and fast."

"Plus there wasn't much of a cool-down period. Our unsub's on a spree." Deidre looked up to see Jackson walk in. "Took you long enough."

"Couldn't get through the traffic. Like yesterday's?"

"Almost exactly, except for the location and the number of notches."

"Does the number mean something?"

"It's a lead." Deidre's phone started beeping. "Tordano." Listening, she pulled out a pad and wrote the information down. "Thanks."

Hanging up, she let out a sigh. "Hope you didn't have any plans for today, 'cause it's going to be a long one."

Jackson looked at her. "What is it now?"

"Emily Lee's body was just found outside of Northridge Mall twenty minutes ago." Deidre turned toward Jessie's body. "We've got a spree killer on the loose."

—

Christmas decorations already appeared outside the mall even though Thanksgiving was still a couple of weeks away. Along the tape, people stood on their tiptoes, showing the odd fascination people seem to have with Deidre's profession.

Parking in the fire lane by the building—the one place there weren't any cars or news vans—Deidre got out. Cameras started to flash and she held up her arm to block her eyes, reaching back in the car to grab her sunglasses.

"Detective!"

"Detective!"

"Detective, is this connected to the murder of the girl from yesterday?"

"Does this have anything to do with the blocked-off street downtown?"

"Does Badge City have a serial killer?"

With a sigh, Deidre made her way to the tape. "No comments at this time. But as soon as information becomes available, I'll be sure to pass it along."

Ducking under, she signed her second crime scene log of the day—a little much for before eight in the morning—and made her way over to where a photographer was documenting the scene.

Once again, the body was curled up, as if the girl was dreaming. A faded comforter covered this victim, allowing several Disney princesses to smile at Deidre. Red hair peeked out from under the comforter and Deidre could see the footie part of her pajamas sticking out the other end.

"Someone tell me something I can use." Deidre went over to find Officer Rogers standing by, writing frantically on a clipboard. "What have we got?"

"She was found by an employee coming in for work. At first, they thought she was lost and had fallen asleep but quickly realized something was wrong."

"Where's the statement?"

"Officer Mason is taking it now." Rogers nodded to an officer who stood by a woman.

"Let me guess; the security camera didn't catch a thing."

"We sent someone to take a look and should have that answer in a few minutes."

Deidre slipped on a pair of gloves and knelt by the body, being sure to place herself between the press and the vic. She turned the victim flat on her back, revealing four notches along her right arm. "What do these mean?"

Deidre made sure to place her body between the press and the arm so that a photograph wouldn't be taken.

Looking up at the entrance, she saw a banner declaring, "American Girl, Opening Soon!"

CHAPTER FOUR

Back at the Station

After stopping to tell two sets of parents the worst news of their lives, Deidre dragged herself back to the station, though she wanted nothing more than to drag herself back into bed and hope that she would wake up from this nightmare.

Stepping into her office, she found her desk overflowing with files. She took a second to pull out evidence boards, then began pinning things up. A summer photo of Grace Miller, the body placement, the number of notches, the information from the interview, the information from the school, and the number on the desk were all up on the board.

Turning, she found the files from the CSU units on the homes of Jessie and Emily. The searchers had found numbers carved into the home desks of both girls. Four in Jessie's and two in Emily's. What did these numbers mean?

It seemed like she was repeating herself when she posted photos for Jessie and then Emily, setting up the places where the rest of the pictures would go as soon as she had them. Her earlier assessment was right, they seemed almost identical. Ten-year-old girls with similar hobbies, activities, grades, lifestyles. But they lived in different parts of town, went to different schools, went to different churches, but did have something else in common.

"Hamilton." She went over to the officer's desk.

"Yes, ma'am?"

"I need a list of every child involved in the Westlake Rec Center soccer league."

Nodding, he turned to his computer. "Consider it done."

Heading back to her desk, she pinned a map of the city to the second board before looking over her notes. Red pins went into the locations of where the girls had lived, and blue represented where their bodies were found. Different colored sharpies linked the right girl to the right scene but still, Deidre didn't see any rhyme or reason.

Correction: she didn't see any rhyme or reason that made the uneasy feeling in her gut go away. "Jackson."

"What's up?" He came over from his desk to look at the board.

"What's similar about the three locations?"

He looked at the board before looking back at her. "They all seem like places you would take your kids. The trail Grace was found on leads to a picnic spot. You have plans to take Mac to the Children's Museum, and Lilly to that same mall."

"So, our unsub has kids?"

"Or doesn't." Jackson took a folder an officer handed him and opened it to reveal the photos from earlier. Deidre took them and put them in the appropriate spots on the evidence board. "Look at the drawing we found at Jessie's scene. It was the first time our unsub tried to speak to us."

"So they're getting revenge for someone losing a child?"

"By taking it out on other families?"

Taking a sip of coffee, Deidre shrugged. "It doesn't have to make sense to us, just to them."

"Running with this, why would a person lose a child?"

"Miscarriage? Lost custody? Still birth? Birth defect? It could be a lot of things" Deidre shrugged.

"So," Jackson headed back to his desk. "Check the records for ten years ago?"

"Yeah. But there's something else."

"Similar?"

"Yet different enough that we might not have caught it." Deidre stood back up and pointed at the pictures. "Look at the bodies."

"We've covered the notches."

"Something else." Deidre studied the photo. "The bodies are covered."

"A sign of remorse? Yet they keep killing."

"But remorse is something. Remorse for the killing or the victims?"

"Maybe regrets playing out in the form of the murders."

"Maybe, but this doesn't help us find the unsub. Whoever this is, they were moving fast. And they might not be done." Deidre plopped down at her desk with a sigh.

A cup sat itself down on her desk. Deidre looked up to find her husband smiling down at her.

"I got them to put an extra shot of expresso in there." Bill held up a bag with take-out in it. "And lunch."

"Have I ever told you I love you?"

"Once or twice. How's it going?"

"Detective!" Hamilton walked over with a slip of paper. "We just got a call from King James Church. There is a child missing, meets the description of our victims."

Deidre looked at Bill. "Does that answer your question? Hamilton!"

"Yes, Detective?"

"I need that list and for you to put an Amber Alert out on..." She grabbed the slip of paper and read it. "...Katelyn Summers. Also, tell King James to lock that church down. No one in, no one out until we get there."

Grabbing her coat, she exchanged a quick kiss with her husband. "Jackson, the research will have to wait. We've got a missing girl and hours to find her alive."

—

THE SIREN WAILED and the lights flashed as Deidre raced through traffic towards King James Church. Something told her, somewhere on that playground, was a number.

And that same something told her she wasn't going to like it.

Making one last turn, she tore into the parking lot, coming to a stop by the front steps of the church. Taking the steps two at a time, she headed for the front door and could hear Jackson frantically trying to follow her. Inside, she found the pastor standing, waiting, pacing, his suit jacket off and sleeves rolled up.

"She was on the playground?"

The pastor nodded. "Her parents say they left her there and returned inside for a reception. We have some missionaries from Africa visiting this week. It's such a nice day out."

The small party took off down the hallway. "Is everyone on lockdown?"

"Yes, no one in or out. We have some in the sanctuary, but most everyone is in the reception hall."

"Find her parents, tell them I'm going to need to talk to them, ASAP. A crime scene unit is on its way. Probably almost here, and they'll need to process the playground."

They arrived at a pair of double doors and Deidre

pushed them open to find an access to the playground. Play equipment filled the area around them, then gave way to a basketball court and—beyond that—a small meadow. The field was lined with trees that hid one side of the chain link fence that surrounded the area.

"Look for a number." Deidre pulled a pair of gloves out of her pocket.

"Those aren't going to do you much good." The pastor's voice came from behind her.

"Why's that?"

"The church has hundreds of members and that means a ton of kids running through here on a regular basis."

"Worth a shot."

Jackson searched the play equipment and she examined the meadow. She stepped over balls, and bubbles, and around a few tricycles that were left at the edge of the court. Circling the court, she found no sign of the elusive number, no sign that this was her guy. The nets on either side were clear as well.

"How's it going over there?" Deidre called to her partner.

She looked over to find him squished into the top of the tower by the slide. "Next jungle gym, you're climbing up," he said.

Deidre grinned. "What are the odds of that happening anytime soon?"

The grass field was clear too, only a few toys scattered around as she made her way to the trees. She checked the first tree, second, third—nothing. She was beginning to wonder if she was wrong.

Finally on the fourth tree's trunk on the side facing the fence, Deidre found a four carved into the side, filled in with red marker—at least she hoped it was marker. Just like the table at the Rec Center and just like in Jessie and Emily's bedrooms.

"I found it." She called to Jackson.

"What number is it?"

"Four." Deidre took off for the doors to the school. "Four."

She walked away from the tree. "Four here, seven, three, eight."

What did they have in common?

COFFEE IN HAND, Deidre walked back into the busy precinct past the mob of reporters who had set up base just outside the precinct. "Jackson, keep looking up those past cases. I think I've got another lead but in the meantime we need to explore all our options."

"Sure thing." He disappeared over to his desk and she made her way into the office where more files waited for her. Taking a quick glance, she found the reports from the earlier crime scenes.

"Hamilton!"

The officer quickly appeared in her doorway. "Yes, ma'am?"

"What's the status on those lists?"

"I'm working on gathering parents' names to run a check now. I should have the rosters on your desk soon."

"Thank you."

The officer quickly made his exit and Deidre added the information to the board, including a picture of Katelyn. Having these four young girls stare back at her, especially with the pictures that accompanied three of them, was unsettling. But there was something, something to give her a lead here somewhere. Shaking away the growing feeling in the pit of her stomach, she tried to figure out her next move.

"Rogers!"

"Yes?" He stood outside, sticking his head in the doorway.

"Have roadblocks been set up?"

"Yes, but so far, nothing."

Nodding, she heard a growl from her stomach, and realized she hadn't eaten breakfast. And the meal her husband had brought was sitting in the fridge in the break room. Heading that direction, she pulled it out, reheated it, and headed back to her desk.

Picking up her phone, she called her husband.

"Find the girl?"

"Not yet, but we're looking for her. Did Lilly get to the game okay?"

"Yes, I walked her in myself."

"Thanks."

"Lilly is fine. You're going to catch this guy."

"I'm glad one of us is confident. I've got three bodies, a fourth one missing and no idea what I'm looking for."

"You and Jackson will figure it out."

She took another bite of food. "But how many more families will lose a daughter before I figure it out?"

"How long can someone keep this pace? Just go with your gut and you'll figure it out. Your dad is with the twins at Lilly's game and Susan's parents are bringing her here to the gym after. Everything is okay here, so worry about those other kids."

"Okay. I might be home real late tonight, if at all."

"Just don't overdo it."

"I won't if our unsub doesn't." She laughed. "Gotta go, maybe something here will tell me where Katelyn is."

Hanging up, she turned in her chair to face the evidence boards. Three bodies, a fourth missing.

She knew that.

Deidre took her tacks out and added in Katelyn's before realizing she was missing a couple. She added in the Rec Center where Grace was taken.

She knew that there were carved marks in each location where the girl was taken from. She also knew there were notches in the arm of each girl.

Was that a coincidence or were the two sets of numbers connected?

Looking at the clock, she realized it was almost one.

Another hour gone.

And she still had no leads on where Katelyn Summers was.

What was she going to tell the family?

Angus appeared on the far side of the bullpen and caught Deidre's eye. He held up a folder and she breathed out a sigh of relief. "I think I've got something."

Deidre pulled up a chair. "It's better than what I've got."

Angus took a seat and handed Deidre the folder. She opened it, laying it on the desk. "I was right, Grace Miller died from blood loss due to the notches in her arm. I was also able to determine that said notches were done with a serrated knife almost like..."

"Almost like what?"

"Almost like the knives hunters use to gut fish and animals. Which makes sense considering."

"Considering what?"

"There's an off smell coming from her arm, and I mean off even for a dead body."

"So I'm assuming you send everything off to the lab, which means I'll know what's causing it in about six months." Deidre leaned back in her chair and not for the first time wished things could go as smoothly for her as they did for the detectives on television.

"You would, if I hadn't cashed in a favor and explained how the bodies of girls are piling up. This isn't definite by any means, detective, but the results indicate that the notches contain bacteria. Bacteria that only exists in the guts of indigenous fish."

"Which means whoever did this works with fish and has low hygiene standards?" Deidre crinkled her nose. "See if I eat seafood anytime soon."

"The lab realized this could be something so they are rushing the preliminary tests on Jessie and Emily as well." Angus added. "But I also included what I've concluded from their preliminary autopsies and I can tell you these were done by the same killer like we suspected."

"If so, we have something else to link them." Turning, she scanned the bullpen. "Rogers!"

"Yes?" He quickly made an appearance.

"I need you to start compiling a list of places where someone could get a knife like this." She turned the page and showed him the rough estimate of what they thought the knife would look like.

Turning back to Angus, she smiled. "Thanks for getting this to me so fast."

"I'm not quite done with the last two yet, but I wanted to bring you these."

"I'm hoping not to have a fourth one for you."

"I wouldn't mind not seeing you for a little bit."

"Gee thanks, Angus."

As he left, Deidre leaned back in her chair and looked at the board. Grabbing the preliminary reports, she added in details. Finally able to fill out a bit of the all-important timeline. Alibis, that is, if they could find a suspect to link an alibi to, could be checked now that they had an idea of the time of death of the three victims.

Grace was last seen around ten. Looking at Angus' time of death window, she could have died six hours later.

Could that be a warning of the timeline?

If so what did the seven mean? There was no way to know for sure when Jessie or Emily were taken, because both sets of parents had gone to bed thinking their girls were safe.

But hypothetically…

Could they be a set of warnings? A way of playing cat and mouse with her? Was the killer really advertising when he was going to kill and kidnap these girls?

If so what did that mean for Katelyn? There was a four on that tree on the playground. Could Katelyn really have less than four hours to live?

Was she right?

It was a theory. But that theory didn't get her any closer to finding the murderer.

Looking at the timelines and the pictures, Deidre tried to wrap her mind around it some more. "So the carvings from where they were taken are when the first victim will be killed and the notches indicate when the next victim will be taken."

Sitting down at her desk, she made a note on the pad that was quickly becoming filled with scribbled notes. Now if she could only figure out what to do with this information.

CHAPTER FIVE

Too Late

"I HAVE YOUR LISTS ma'am."

Deidre looked up and saw Rogers holding out a file.

"I'm running names now for the parents but thought you would want to take a look."

"Thank you, Rogers."

As Rogers left her office, an idea hit and she opened her email to find the one the rec center had sent her the other day regarding Lily's upcoming tournament.

Opening the email, she looked at the bracket, then printed a copy to follow up on a hunch. Running to the printer, she grabbed it and went back. Grabbing the first list—Grace Miller's team, the Red Wings—she circled Grace's name before writing it over the team on the bracket.

The next team, Silver Linings, was free from victims so far. Deidre set it aside, ready to do something if she was right.

The Yellow Rays were next and, not for the first time, she wondered who on Earth it was who came up with these names. Katelyn Summers' name was on that list, so Deidre added it to the bracket.

White Warriors were next, and once again Deidre sent up a prayer of thanks her daughter wasn't on that team so she didn't have to deal with those white uniforms. This list was also victim-free, but the feeling in the pit of her stomach said that it might be a matter of time before that changed.

Gold Stars were next, and the butterflies in her stomach did a dance as she saw her daughter's name along the roster. Such connections were driving her a bit nuts and Deidre once again almost reached for her phone to check on her.

"She's okay, she's at school. She'll be fine." Deidre let out a deep breath and put that list together with the two that didn't have victims yet.

Green Goals revealed Jessie Phillips' name, so it was added to the bracket, followed quickly by Emily Lee representing the Maroon Mavericks.

That left the Blue Lagoons along with the Stars, Linings, and Warriors.

Half the bracket was filled, the other half wasn't.

Taking the lists, she headed over to Rogers' desk. "While the checks are running, can you find me some contact info, preferably email, for these? You can get it from Lexi Lestrade at the Rec Center. Actually, while you're talking to her, ask her to come in."

Feeling like she was at least making progress, she chanced a look at the clock and realized there wasn't a lot of time left in the search for Katelyn Summers. She had leads but no solid clues as to where the girl might be.

That led to other questions.

Going back to her evidence board, Deidre studied the pictures. None of the victims had been killed where their bodies were placed. Which meant they had scenes for body dumps, but no idea where the murders actually took place. Where were the true *scenes* of the crimes?

Glancing at the report on her desk, she wondered if that fish thing really was something. Granted that narrowed it down some, but not a whole lot. With miles of coastline stretching down one side of the city, who knew how many boats and fisherman there were out there?

Well someone knew, but she had a feeling she didn't have time to wait for that kind of information.

Unless…

Unless it wasn't a fisherman.

Following the map with her finger, Deidre traced a stretch of land by the ocean. Processing plants lined this area, serving commercial fisherman eager to get their catch from their boats to restaurants across the country. And they would have knives like the one Angus said.

But most were automatic now, having cut jobs to save money thanks to the recession. In fact, a few closed because they went under allowing vacant buildings to sit abandoned in a once-vibrant area.

But knives, numbers, timelines, what if they were connected? What if the numbers led to bodies or to the next kidnapping?

Deidre paused at the board and looked, working off a timeline that relied on Angus' approximate time of death for Grace. But was it feasible that the number of notches lined up to when Jessie was kidnapped to have her at the Children's Museum during the blackout?

But that would mean…

A shadow crossed her desk and she looked up to see Jackson.

"They found Katelyn."

—

THE WIND BLEW the swings back and forth across the empty playground as officers rolled out crime scene tape, sealing the area off from the rest of the world.

Pulling her trench coat close, Deidre stepped out of the car and breathed in the cold, salty air. Definitely not something she would ever grow tired of.

That was not something that could be said about the sight that waited for her on the playground. An old-fashioned wooden jungle gym, a rarity in this world of plastic and metal, stood a couple stories high. Fort-like in its appearance, it served as that or a castle, depending on who occupied it.

"Where's the body?" Deidre turned to Hamilton who was taking statements from a family. Two small children crowded close to their parents.

Hamilton pointed up. "Like Rapunzel in her tower."

"You've got to be kidding me." She turned to the playground. Sure enough, she could see the camera flashes coming from the top. Turning to Jackson she nodded. "So we've got an unsub who was able to carry a kid to the top of the jungle gym?"

"Using the rope ladder in the back it's not that hard. He could have rigged a pulley system."

"Which means our unsub is familiar enough with the area. They would have to be to get in here in the middle of the day like this, without being seen."

"Face it; after Labor Day, this park isn't used a whole lot."

"Well, shall we?" Deidre went around to the back and was glad she hadn't worn heels, another thing she couldn't understand from the TV shows. You would think they would get tired of doing takes in those heels and get the memo—but no...

"You said the next jungle gym is yours," Jackson reminded her.

"I seriously didn't think that I would have to pay up this soon."

Shaking her head, she climbed up the rope ladder. When she was at the top, she got her first look at the dead body. A backpack lay beside her, just like with Grace Miller. Like the others it was laid so that, if Deidre didn't know any better, she would have thought the girl was taking a nap, truly a princess locked away in the tower waiting for her prince to come. Rapunzel was an accurate nickname as the Asian girl's long black hair seemed to mirror the fairy tale princess.

But no prince would come and Katelyn wouldn't awaken. Deidre moved up onto the ledge and allowed Jackson up, careful not to get in the way of the Crime Scene Unit as they processed the small scene. The photographer stepped away and nodded to Deidre who took a look at the body.

"Thought this was mine."

"And let you have all the fun?"

Sure enough, there were notches, just one this time, in the right arm of the girl.

"Anything in the backpack?"

"Just her soccer cleats, the latest American Girl, and traditional school stuff. Nothing that suggests that she had any idea that this was about to happen."

"Wait." Deidre stopped cold looking at Jackson. "You're looking through her backpack."

"Yeah, from what your report said, it was the same way with Grace Miller."

"Except that, with Grace, she was abducted inside the rec center where she had been working on homework. Katelyn was at church."

"Could she have had it with her?"

"We can check."

"I'm getting too old for this." Angus' disgruntled cry could be heard up there.

Heading over to the ledge she looked down to see him standing there, arms crossed. "Do you think I want to be up here?"

"Yeah, but you've got a few less years on you." He grunted as he began the climb up, nodding to his assistants. "Figure out how to get this body down because I'm not going to carry it down bridal style."

"Come on, Angus. Where's your sense of adventure?" Deidre held out her hand and helped him up on the platform.

"This our guy?"

"Yeah, just one notch. I think he's done messing around."

Angus slipped on a pair of gloves before coming over to the body. "No hesitation. Whoever this is—he's gotten comfortable doing this."

"Could he be attempting to evolve? Or reach endgame?"

"Sadly, the only way to know that is to find more bodies. This unsub has evolved a bit since Grace Miller yesterday. There was hesitation there, almost an uncertainty. Now he thinks he's either doing the right thing or what needs to be done."

Letting out a sigh, Deidre knelt next to the body and looked at Jackson, who was kneeling on the other side. "Something tells me we're only halfway through this mess."

—

"Detective?" Mrs. Miller greeted Deidre as she reentered the station, her face evidence enough of how rough of a night it had been. "I heard there's been more girls."

Deidre put a hand on her shoulder. "We're doing

everything we can to figure out who's behind this. Is there anything I can do for you?"

Mr. Miller stepped up. "We want to see her."

"Are you sure?" Deidre needed to give them the option.

"I need to see my baby."

She nodded to the lady behind the front desk. "Jackie, can you call Angus and tell him I'm on the way with the Miller family?"

Jackie nodded and Deidre led the way out.

"How did you get here?"

"Officer Hamilton stopped by and gave us a ride."

Nodding, she opened the door to her car and held it open for the Miller family. "Where's Lucy?"

"With her grandparents."

They slid into the car and Deidre shut the door before getting in and heading down to Angus' office. The drive, which usually felt long enough because of the nature of her visits, felt even longer with the two pairs of eyes going into the back of her head. She tried to make small talk, but it fizzled out before a real conversation could begin.

None of their hearts were in it.

They pulled into Angus' office and found him waiting at the door. Deidre got out and held open the door. "They wanted to come and see their daughter."

Angus nodded. "I have her ready to view."

He turned to the family. "Mr. And Mrs. Miller, I'm so sorry for your loss. I'm Dr. Angus Ramsey. I performed the autopsy on Grace. If you have any questions, feel free to ask."

"Can we see her?"

Angus nodded. "If you'll follow me."

Deidre followed them into the building. Knowing the nature of his job, Angus tried to keep it well-lit, cheerful.

But once you passed the front areas, the dark, dank feeling that accompanied the dead seemed to seep through the pores of the walls themselves.

Angus led them down a long hallway finally stopping at a door. "I placed her in here. Take all the time you need but I have to ask that you don't touch her. The smallest touch could contaminate the evidence."

"I'll be right out here with Dr. Ramsey if you need anything."

The couple made their way into the room and Deidre stood beside Angus at the one-way mirror in order to watch them, yet let them have their space to grieve.

For a minute, they seemed to hover by the door as if second guessing themselves. Mrs. Miller turned into Mr. Miller, positioning herself so her face was turned away from the body. Thanks to a speaker, they could hear the conversation.

"Is it her?"

A sigh could be heard over the intercom. "It is, Steph."

No matter how many times she had to watch this scene play out, Deidre never seemed to be able to distance herself from it.

Mrs. Miller turned, and Deidre saw the moment when she absorbed the fact that it was truly her daughter lying on the steel table in front of her. She watched as, with hesitant footsteps, Mrs. Miller made her way forward, brushing the stray hair that had fallen across Grace's face.

"My baby."

Mrs. Miller seemed to almost fall to the ground, using her husband and the edge of the table to keep her semi-upright. "Oh, my poor baby."

Sobs filled the room as her husband pulled her upright and consoled her, tears running down his face as well.

"I hate having to watch parents grieve." Angus finally spoke up. "A parent should never have to bury their child."

"Especially ones so young." Deidre turned to him. "While I'm here, have the results come back?"

Angus nodded. "Let me run to my office and grab them. I was about to head your way when your secretary called."

Deidre nodded, sensed the ticking of a clock she knew she couldn't stop. Kids were disappearing faster than she could figure it out, and she had no idea how to find this killer.

Leads were one thing, but none of them were what she would call solid. None of them had enough evidence that could point somewhere.

Watching the Miller family mourn in the room, Deidre couldn't help but let out a sigh. She had four bodies, a gut feeling that a fifth wouldn't be too long away, and no solid links besides the soccer league.

But with each team having fifteen or so kids, that was almost sixty potential targets. Though in a city the size of this one, that was a relatively small number.

But still.

How was this person picking these kids from these teams? The socioeconomics were different, the races were different, their schools were different, and the geographic locations of the bodies were different.

Their age was the only thing in common. Well, maybe Jackson would find something.

But with only one notch on Katelyn Summers' arm, Deidre felt like they would still be too late.

CHAPTER SIX

Cold Case

THIS WHOLE CASE made her think about Lilly, her daughter, and every time she looked at the tournament brackets, all she could see was her daughter's team.

"Deidre?"

She looked up to see Jackson standing over her desk, files in hand. "I found a few possible leads."

Opening the top one, she noticed the coffee stain on its corner and wondered if it was hers before scanning the first page. "We've got a couple unsolved homicides—oh, I remember that one." She flipped to another file. "What's this? A rape that wasn't investigated? Why is this here?"

"It's far enough back that if a baby was born, it would be about ten years old. But this case is really politics at its worst." Jackson nodded at the file. "And you know the victim."

"Who?"

"Lexi Lestrade. Who's waiting in the lobby, by the way? Something about you wanting to see her?"

"Yeah, I got Rogers to call her in." Grabbing the file, she stood up. "Let me take this into the conference room."

Heading out to the lobby, she found Alexandria "Lexi" Lestrade sitting on a bench. She had a copy of today's paper in her hands, an article about the recent elections on the front page. Outside the station's door, she could see the press juggling for the best spot to get a photo.

Deidre positioned herself so they couldn't see Lexi. "Budget troubles?"

Lexi lowered the paper to look at Deidre. "Not yet, but let this victory cool off for these guys."

"Thanks for coming in. I really appreciate it. Sorry about the zoo out there, they mean well."

"It's okay, I just want to do whatever I can do to help, Detective." Lexi stood up. "Is Lilly ready for the tournament?"

"She's about to bounce off the walls." Deidre stayed behind her as they made their way to the conference room. "I need to ask you a few questions."

They both took a seat. "About?"

"Several things, but first," Deidre put the file down on the table. "What happened almost ten years ago and why wasn't it investigated?"

Lexi's face went real pale, real fast.

—

Valentine's Day – 2004

Lexi stood in front of the mirror gently swaying back and forth, back and forth, allowing the royal blue dress she'd bought to just swish around.

He'd be there soon.

As she pinned on her jewelry, she tapped her foot to the pop music she had playing. It had finally happened. Steven

Richards had finally asked her out. The guy she'd had a crush on since freshman year had finally asked her out.

He wouldn't tell her where they were going, only that it would be a special evening. Not that an evening with him would not be special! After all, he was the star quarterback, heading off to play for Notre Dame in the fall. Said he wanted to study Political Science and maybe even become president someday.

First Lady.

Lexi shook her head: they hadn't even had their first date yet, and here she was thinking about the future. Not that she could help it. A quick glance at her desk told her that the acceptance letter to the University of California on a full soccer scholarship promised her the beginning of that bright future.

And it was all just a few short months away.

Downstairs, the doorbell rang and she heard her father answer it. Grabbing her handbag, she made her way downstairs and found him waiting.

Tonight was going to be perfect.

—

LEXI LOOKED AWAY for a second, signs of a painful memory clear on her face. "I was so young then."

"What happened, Lexi?"

"Everything was fine during dinner. He took me to a fancy Italian place, was a perfect gentlemen. Then afterwards, he wanted to go for a walk on the beach."

—

THE WAVES CRASHED beside them as they walked hand in hand along the beach. Ahead, Lexi could see another couple doing the same thing and couldn't help but smile at Steven. "I had a wonderful time tonight."

"I'm glad."

They continued walking until they were by the pier and when they reached it, Steven took her other hand and turned her so she was facing him. "Have I told you that you look really beautiful tonight, Lexi?"

Lexi felt heat rush to her cheeks. "Thanks."

He pressed her hard up against the pier, kissing her so hard her head snapped against the wood. He pulled away for just a second before kissing her again, and again, each one harder than the last.

"What are you doing?"

"Showing you how beautiful you look tonight." He pulled her closer, something Lexi hadn't thought was possible, and his hands moved down her back.

"That's enough."

"What's wrong, Lexi?"

"I said, that's enough."

"Well, I say we're not quite done."

—

DEIDRE HELD UP a tissue to the crying woman. Lexi took it, blew her nose, and set out a sigh. "He, he kept telling me I was beautiful and then he did it and afterwards he took me home like nothing happened."

"What happened next?"

"I told my parents. Oh the look on my mom's face." Lexi grabbed another tissue. "She was so angry and hurt, and scared. We came down to the station; I think your father took the report."

Deidre double checked the report and sure enough, her father's signature was there. Daniel Brighton.

"But then nothing happened. Sure, there were a couple days where they looked like they were investigating and then nothing. And then…"

"Then what?"

"Then, Mayor Richards came to the house just after I found out I was pregnant. Mom was so shocked and angry that she had the nerve to come talk to me after what her son did. And she…"

"She what?"

"She wanted me to get rid of the baby." Lexi grabbed another tissue, blowing her nose into it. "She offered to pay me to have an abortion."

"Did you?"

"No, I couldn't. I just… I couldn't."

"What did the mayor say?"

"She offered to pay for me to go to college after I had the baby, if I would keep who the father was silent."

"And did you take the deal?"

"I didn't want to—I wanted him to suffer. But she offered to pay for school and the economy was already awful and that would be one less thing my parents had to worry about, especially since I was going to lose my scholarship when they found out I was pregnant."

"What happened to the baby?"

The tears started again, and it took Deidre several minutes to calm her down. For now, she decided to drop the subject but she still had more questions.

"Did Steven ever know he was a father?"

"I mean, he's a father now." Lexi scoffed. "And after yesterday, he's well on his way to living the life he always wanted."

"What do you mean?"

Lexi held up the paper, showing Deidre the front page.

"He was elected to office in Sacramento. They're saying he's on track to be one of the youngest Governors in state history. That's what he wanted—to be Governor and then on to President. I used to dream of what it would be like to be his First Lady. I was so stupid…"

Deidre put a hand on Lexi's shoulder. "I have a few more questions for you—can you handle it?"

Lexi nodded.

"Who has access to the rosters for the league?"

"Anyone that works at the rec center. Is this about those girls?" Lexi pointed to another story. Sure enough, Grace was on the front page and Lexi pointed to it. "I can't believe someone would do that to the girls in my league."

"Your league? You mentioned that the other day—something about budget cuts?"

Lexi nodded. "I coordinate the leagues now. They wanted to get rid of some due to budget cuts, but I fought for them. That's why we did the fundraisers over the summer. We raised some of the money needed to keep going and it held the city off from shutting us down."

"Can you make a list of people who would have access?" Deidre slid a pad of paper to her. "Give it to Officers Hamilton or Jackson, and then call me if you remember anything."

Deidre walked out of the conference room and went to grab her keys. Just as she was out the door, Jackson stopped her. "We think we found girl number five. A family just reported their little girl missing."

CHAPTER SEVEN

Natalie

"MOM? WHAT ARE you doing here?"

Deidre looked around as she entered the rec center yet again. The main room was filled with girls who were wearing a variety of sweats and shorts. Several soccer balls rolled back and forth across the floor.

Not too far from the door was Lilly, who got up from where she had been sitting with her friends and ran over.

Lilly nodded to the gun at her mother's side. "You're on duty."

"I am."

"Is it about Natalie?"

"Do you know her?"

Lilly shook her head. "Not really, she played for the Blue Lagoons. So I met her a few times when we played each other this season. I just heard people talking about her. Is it true? Is she missing? Is it like the other girls?"

Deidre knelt down in front of her daughter. "Uncle Jackson and I are doing everything we can to stop this person. You don't need to worry about it, okay?"

"Okay." Lilly looked over Deidre's shoulder. "Hi, Uncle Jackson."

"Hey, Lilly." Her partner came and wrapped her daughter in a hug.

"Now go back to your friends and we're going to get back to work, okay?"

Lilly nodded and ran back to her friends.

Straightening up, Deidre glanced around the center. "Where was Natalie last seen?"

"Her parents dropped her by the door so she could change." Jackson took the clipboard from one of the officers, turning it so he could read it. "Practice started a few minutes later but she never came out of the locker room. Her mother went to check on her and found her school clothes on the bench."

"Number?"

"Under the clothes."

"Locker room?"

"Yeah."

Deidre took off, the sound of footsteps echoing behind her letting her know that Jackson was following her. In the locker room she met a tornado of clothes, backpacks, perfumes, accessories, hygiene products.

"And they say boys are messy." Jackson muttered.

"Where was Natalie's stuff?"

"According to the report, over here." Jackson's voice echoed off the walls of the locker room as he moved past Deidre and went down one of the aisles. "They're labeled by teams."

Deidre stopped at the aisle that had a gold star on the side and walked down it, pausing when she saw Lilly's name on a gold star. Snapping out of her thoughts, she made her way back to the main aisle before finding Jackson, taking care not to step on any of the stuff that seemed to be littered about everywhere.

Finally she saw a blue star and ducked under the crime tape that blocked the aisle.

"You realize we're going to have a group of girls telling their teachers that the police took their homework?"

"Wonder how that'll go over?" Jackson laughed.

Chuckling, Deidre made her way to where Jackson stood. Looking down, she saw a three carved into the bench, once again filled in with red marker.

"Jackson?" A thought came to mind that did nothing for the feeling deep in her gut.

"Yeah?"

"Did we ever test the marker at any of the locations?"

"We sent it in, but don't have the results. Why?"

"What if it's not marker?"

—

IT TOOK TIME before Deidre could leave the rec center, but instead of heading back to the station, she had another stop in mind. She turned down a familiar street, and pulled into the driveway of the house she grew up in.

Letting herself in the side door, Deidre heard the sound of *Phineas and Ferb* playing on the TV.

"Whatcha doing?" The voice came from the TV.

Chuckling to herself, she made her way past the den where she could see the heads of her two youngest, content to be watching the antics of the cartoon boys. She headed toward the kitchen where she could smell the beginnings of dinner.

She walked in to see her mom and dad in the kitchen, working seamlessly together to make dinner. Her dad noticed her first. "Deidre, when did you get here?"

"Just walked in. Can I ask you something?"

Her face must have given away the seriousness of the situation because he nodded. "Sure, do you want to go in my office?"

She nodded and he led the way to the familiar office at the back of the house.

"That bad?"

"I didn't say anything yet."

"You didn't have to. I saw the paper this morning and I just watched the news. You've got four girls dead and rumor has it there's a fifth one missing."

"It's more than a rumor, Dad."

Daniel groaned. "And they're all Lilly's age?"

Deidre nodded. "And part of the same soccer league as Lilly. I can't help it but I see her every time I have to look at the body of yet another girl that this unsub has decided to end for no reason whatsoever."

"There's a reason."

"Why would you kill innocent girls?"

"I didn't say it was a logical reason. It doesn't have to make sense to us as long as it makes sense to him."

"But it seems like every time I get a possible answer, I end up with even more questions."

"Talk to me, Deidre."

Deidre spent the next few minutes explaining the case to him, the fish bacteria located on the notches, the notches themselves and how the current theory was that they had to do with time. Notches on the arm meant time until the next girl went missing, the numbers left behind told them how much time that girl had left.

"I'm questioning that instead of being colored in with marker, that maybe these numbers are colored in with blood."

"Where would she have gotten the blood for the first number?"

"Her own? Maybe it wasn't human and could have something to do with the fish thing. You know how the lab is; we might not know for ages. Even the fish thing isn't a sure thing. That was a preliminary test." Deidre ran her hands through her hair. "But there's something else bothering me."

"What?"

"Valentine's Day 2004, you took the statement of a girl who claimed that the mayor's son raped her. The case was investigated but never followed through. Why?"

Her dad sighed. "You're talking about Alexandria Lestrade, aren't you?"

Deidre nodded.

"There are things that happen, things that are out of my control. By that time, I was Chief of Detectives and you were a detective and had just had Mac. But when Alexandra came in, all I could see was my little girl. It drove me nuts that I couldn't follow through. She had proof. Medical proof. That girl lost everything because of that garbage and no one will ever know better."

"Why couldn't you follow through?"

"It was an election year, it was the mayor's son, and my job was threatened. I was so close to earning retirement, and you had a family and I couldn't drag you into this. I... regret it. I was a coward. Can you imagine your granddad doing that?"

"The mayor threatened the department, didn't she?"

"Not directly. But I think she ended up paying Lexi off 'cause the charges were dropped. And I don't think that was Steven's first rape—or his last. I always waited for another chance to pin him, on anything, and use some friends in the DA to push toward a lifetime in prison. Nothing ever came into my hands. He has enough money to buy whatever—and whoever—he wants."

"Didn't he just get elected to office last week? And still?"

Another nod met her. "I believe so. And the whole time, I couldn't say anything. I retired, and there was never anything to go on. I hoped he'd fade, like the rest of my ghosts. And then I had to pick up the paper this morning and see his face all over the front page." He swallowed.

Deidre caught a look at the time and got up. "I've got to get back to the station. Thanks for watching Carrie and Connor."

"Not a problem." Her dad opened the door and led her out. "Take some dinner with you. It's better than takeout."

They made their way back into the kitchen where her mom was putting dinner on the table. A bag sat on the counter. "Here you go, dear."

"Thanks, Mom."

"Mommy!" Twin cries reached her ears seconds before matching lumps attached themselves to her legs. "What are you doing here?"

"Mommy had to ask Grandpa a question."

"Are you catching a bad guy?"

"I'm trying to. You be good for Grandma and Grandpa." Hugging them one last time, she grabbed the bag before making her way out to the car and, not for the first time, was thankful there was a Starbucks with a drive-thru on the way back to the police station.

She was going to need it.

—

SHE ARRIVED BACK at the station and saw that it was still a bustle of activity. The press was camped in their usual place by the door and she had to fight her way through to get inside.

"Detective!"

"Is it true there is now a fifth girl missing?"

"Are you any closer to finding the Notches Killer?"

Deidre made a mental note to get the PIO out there quick. Inside, it wasn't much better as various departments worked together in a frenzy.

"Deidre!"

"Detective!"

"Ma'am!"

Jackson, Rogers, and Hamilton all reached her at the same time. All three were holding files.

"If any of you are here to tell me we have a fifth body, please step away."

All three remained in front of her.

"Good. Okay, Jackson, you first."

"I did a little more digging into the cold case angle and found some interesting details about Lexi." He handed her the file. "First off, she got pregnant from the rape and lost her scholarship. She went to a junior college and double majored in athletic training and business management and came back and the then mayor gave her job in order to keep her quiet."

"What happened to the baby?"

"Still trying to figure that out. I've got the hospital pulling the record now."

"If the baby was even born here. Cross-reference any men in her life that might have been or are close enough to go to these lengths."

Jackson nodded.

"Okay, Rogers."

"I did a search on the knives and one store says that our

killer is probably using an industrial knife from a catering catalogue. Old school cannery was his thoughts. So I'm doing some digging into the businesses that shut down due to the recession and should have that report in a couple hours. Unfortunately, a lot of the stores I could contact have closed for the day and I'm going to have to wait for the morning before getting in touch with them."

Taking the second file, Deidre nodded. "And, Hamilton."

"Using the list Detective Jackson provided, I've been running it against the parents of the kid in the league. There hasn't been any that have dinged yet but I've still got a few to go."

Deidre took the third file. "Well, looks like we're all earning our overtime." Deidre took the third file. "Thanks guys, any word on Natalie?"

"Nothing yet. Road blocks are set up; town's on high alert. We were the lead story on the six o clock news tonight."

"So I heard." Deidre took the files and headed to her desk.

Nothing stood out.

But that's why they ran background checks.

Running her hands through her hair, she picked up the file on Lexi. It seemed every time she learned more about the story, the more heartbreaking it was.

And the guy ran for public office and won.

How messed up was that?

Hopefully something would turn up in Jackson's search for the baby. She could see him hunched over his keyboard, eyes glued to the monitor as he scanned the records to find something—anything—that would help them make sense of this.

Glancing at the clock, she realized that Lilly had

probably been picked up and Mac arrived home. Picking up her phone, she dialed Bill. “Are Lilly and Mac okay?”

“Doing fine. We picked up a pizza for dinner and Mac is working on his homework as we speak. Lilly was playing with her dolls last I checked. Said something about mommy taking her homework?”

Deidre couldn’t help but laugh at the comment. “Crime scene. She’s not far off. Can I talk to them?”

Footsteps could be heard on the other end. “It’s your mom.”

“Hi, Mom.” Lilly’s voice came over the phone. “Are you coming home soon?”

“Not quite. How was the rest of practice?”

“They ended up canceling it. They wouldn’t let us go back in the locker room, though, so I can’t do my homework.”

“I’m sure your teacher will understand. Something tells me we’re going to be writing a lot of notes about this for everyone. Are you ready for the tournament?” Deidre pulled the roster, now up to five names on the brackets.

“I think so. Hey, Daddy told me to ask you. Can I spend the night at Audrey’s house Friday? Her birthday is tomorrow and her mom said she can have the whole team over.”

Deidre looked at the calendar and checked the date. “Are you getting a ride home from practice with her?”

“I’m pretty sure, but I can check tomorrow.”

“I don’t think it should be a problem. Do we need to go buy a present?”

“Yeah.”

“Do you know what you want to get her?”

“No…”

Deidre laughed at the way her daughter’s voice trailed off. “Well think about it and when I wrap this up we’ll go shopping.”

"Good, 'cause Daddy's bad at this kind of thing."

"I'll do my best, sweetheart."

"Okay. Love you, Mommy."

"Love you, Lils." She heard the phone exchange hands and footsteps sound on the hardwood floor of the hallway as rock music grew louder. A knock sounded and she knew her son was working away and wouldn't hear for a few more bangs.

"Mac, your mom is on the phone."

The music stopped and the door opened as she heard the phone exchange hands. "Hey, Mom."

"Hey, Mac. How were auditions?"

"I think they went well."

"Do you think you got in?"

"Probably just in the chorus. Sixth graders usually don't get big parts."

"You have to start somewhere."

"Yeah. I heard they found a body at the Children's Museum."

"You shouldn't be worrying about those kinds of things."

"My mom chases bad guys and one is killing girls a lot like my sister."

"How do you know that?"

"They were talking about it in school today."

"Who?"

"Kids. You haven't caught the guy, have you?"

"We're working on it kid, but it's not like those TV shows you insist on watching."

"I know. We still on for this weekend?"

"As soon as Lilly gets out of soccer practice Saturday we're going. Might even do lunch out."

"Really?"

"Really." Deidre smiled. "Love you, kid."

"Love you too, Mom." Deidre heard the door shut and a few seconds passed before her husband picked up again. "How was work?"

"Doing good. Got a few of the kids preparing for a boxing tournament in Sacramento in a couple of weeks."

She looked at her calendar and saw the dates. "That's right."

"You doing okay?"

"Not looking forward to this late night but got a few leads." Deidre looked at the mess of files that was her desk.

"Hang in there okay?"

"Will do. Love you. Call me if anything comes up."

"Love you too."

They ended the call and Deidre sat her phone on her desk, letting out a sigh before she pulled another file off her desk and began reading.

CHAPTER EIGHT

Another Found, Another Missing

THE SUN WAS setting as the phone on Deidre's desk rang, flashing the number of her husband's cell. Curious, she picked up the phone, setting down the file she'd been reading.

"Mommy?" Lilly's voice rang out as Deidre's heart jumped into her throat.

"Lilly? What's wrong?"

"Daddy said I had to call you but, there's a candlelight vigil happening at the Rec Center. The girls from the soccer league are going, and I want to go and can I go?"

"Wait, there's a vigil?" She checked the clock and saw that it was 7:30, about ninety minutes, give or take, until Natalie's time was up.

That is, if the unsub kept to their schedule.

"Yeah, at eight at the Rec Center."

Checking the clock again, she grabbed her jacket and sent a quick prayer up that all lights would be green between the station and there. "I'm on my way to get you and we'll all go together, okay?"

"Okay. See you soon."

The phone clicked as she knocked her knuckles against Jackson's desk. "Get moving! There's a candlelight vigil for the victims in a half hour at the rec center and you know what that means."

He grabbed his jacket and followed her out. "Meet you there."

"Yeah." She turned back to the bull pen. "Rogers! Hamilton! Peters!"

"Yes ma'am!"

"Head to the Rec Center. There's a vigil happening. Watch the crowd 'cause our unsub might be there." She ran out of the center and hopped into her car, paging dispatch to send more men to the site.

Hopefully there would be another piece of the puzzle.

—

WHEN DEIDRE PULLED into the Rec Center, a large crowd had already gathered. Already, candles flickered in the early night. Off to one side, a memorial of sorts began to form.

Walking over, Deidre took a look at the pictures of the four girls smiling back at her. Flowers, stuffed animals, notes, and soccer balls lay around what had been the announcement boards. As she stood there, Lilly and a few other girls came by and laid a gold star on the memorial.

The Millers stood nearby accepting condolences. Around the area, the other families gathered, doing much the same. Along with four families, there were eight other groups that quickly became noticeable, as they were all in their soccer uniforms. Four teams stood near their corresponding parents, an extension of grief.

Deidre made her way back to the collection of gold uniforms and found her husband standing near Lily. His eyes barely left her.

The squeal of a microphone hushed the crowd. Nearby, Deidre saw a small stage that had been built and saw Lexi take front stage, her eyes puffy with tears. "Thank you all for coming tonight. Over the last twenty-four hours, our little community has suffered the loss of four bright young girls and there is a fifth in harm's way."

Deidre couldn't help but let her eyes wander to Natalie's parents.

"But let us all take a minute to thank the members of the police force who have been working tirelessly to put a stop to these acts."

A round of applause rang out and she felt eyes on her as the parents nearby found a focus for their thanks. Shifting her weight, she nodded.

"Lakeview Christian School's choir have come to sing for us tonight." Lexi moved to the side as a group of high schoolers came together.

Before they could start singing, a candle was placed in Deidre's hand as someone offered to light it. She took the flame, passed it on to the next parent beside her. Around her, flames flickered as a hushed silence settled over them.

Amazing Grace
How sweet the sound
That saved a wretch
Like me
I once was lost
But now I'm found
Was blind but now
I see

A large majority of the crowd joined in with the classic hymn as the choir continued on to the next verse. She spotted the press, who had relegated themselves off to the side, either because it offered a better shot or out of respect—it honestly depended on the reporter's integrity.

But the lights that flashed towards the crowd, blocking out parts of the parking lot from sight, couldn't help but remind her that thousands of people in the city were watching this play out. The grief these four—well, five since Natalie's family didn't know one way or another yet—families felt was being put on display and Deidre couldn't help but feel sorry for them.

She moved away from her family, carefully cradling the candle in her hand, and continued walking, observing the crowd of people that seemed to grow with each passing minute.

When we've been there
Ten thousand years
Bright shining as the sun
We've no less days
To sings God's praise
Then when we first begun.

We've no less days
To sing God's praise
Then when we first begun

From somewhere, the sound of a guitar joined the choir and Mrs. Miller took the stage, a framed picture of Grace in hand. She went up to the microphone and it squealed as she adjusted it.

"My name is Stephanie Miller and my daughter, Grace,

was the first victim of this tragedy." There was a pause as she sat the picture on the stage, the girl's smiling face looking out onto the crowd. She pulled a tissue out of her pocket and wiped her eyes, sniffling before she continued.

"I did some reading. They…they say that a lot of times, the person responsible comes to events like this. If you are out there, please stop." She had to stop again. "Please, don't hurt another girl. No family should have to suffer like this."

"When Grace was little, we would come here on Saturday mornings so she could watch the 'big kids' play soccer. She was so excited when we told her that this year she could finally play in the league."

The sob she let out could be heard thanks to the microphone as she turned away. A few minutes later, another person stepped up and shared a story about Jessie. Deidre walked through the crowd as people came up and shared stories. The crowd grew as time went on and the single guitar had turned into a small band.

Just as Emily's older sister was sharing about a vacation they had taken a few months ago, a scream sounded out across the crowd. Deidre took off towards the sound and to her surprise, the crowd seemed to make a path for her.

Looking towards the source, she found four teenagers standing there, backs against the side of the building, staring at a lumpy bundle on the ground.

They had no idea what sneaking away would get them. Four kids who just wanted a good time.

Slowing her steps, she took a look at the scene and realized that if Natalie was that lump, then her whole scene was compromised and she would get nothing from it. Even the tarp would be compromised because of a group of teens who let their hormones take over.

But the look on the girls' faces told her that they had no idea.

Officer Hamilton arrived at her side and took out his pad. "Do you want me to get the couples' statements?"

"Yeah, Rogers should be here and he can take one." She grabbed a pair of gloves and knelt down next to the tarp. The hair stuck out, matching that of the picture she had of Natalie.

Grabbing her radio, she punched in the frequency to Dispatch. "This is Detective Tordano. I've got an 11-44 at the Westlake Rec Center."

"10-4, Detective."

Deidre took in the scene, not wanting to touch anything before the photographer arrived. Jackson arrived after an apparent pit stop at his car because he was already rolling out crime scene tape to block the area off from the ceremony.

But the ceremony ground to a halt as the crowd gathered around the tape, trying to catch a glimpse of the lump laying on the ground.

"Back up! I need everyone to back up!" Jackson must have found a megaphone somewhere and yelled through it, trying to be heard over the crowd's nervous chatter.

Deidre knelt down and peeled the tarp back just enough to see inside and sure enough found herself face to face with Natalie.

She replaced the tarp and walked around the scene, searching the ground for anything that might help figure out who would be bold enough to leave a body a few feet from where a vigil was being held.

—

DEIDRE CHUGGED A Five Hour Energy along with another

sip of coffee and tried to piece together something that would make all of this make sense.

Somewhere was the last piece of the puzzle.

Maybe it was in the victims' files.

As each body had been discovered, a new file had been made, all of which now occupied one corner of her desk. Starting with Grace Miller, she opened each file. Inside she found job histories of both of Grace's parents, where they went to school, Grace's own school records, the date the Millers bought their house, background checks on both parents, and whatever else their analyst had been able to find.

The same process was repeated for Jessie, Emily, Natalie, and Katelyn.

But still nothing stood out. All five families had lived in the area for years but worked different jobs, went to different churches, sent their children to different schools… the only thing she saw that thy had in common was the Rec Center.

Which had been around for as long as she could remember. She used to hang out there when she was little.

It was going on midnight and so far, Natalie's crime scene was proving to be all but useless (the only semi-productive thing it did was link the killer to another victim) but, on the upside, so far no more missing children had been discovered. What she was worried about was having another crazy morning in about six hours—when people started waking up to start the day only to realize they were starting one of the worst days of their lives.

Patrols were increased, and as much of the city as possible was covered. This force was earning their overtime.

But was it enough?

Sitting back in her chair, she tried to hold back a yawn, but it was no use.

In the corner, the radio kept its steady chatter—a reminder that the rest of the world was going on despite the craziness that had overtaken Deidre's own.

"10-51 off of McKinley Road."

"Got a 459 at Anderson Jewelers."

And off and on the radio went, officers darting past her office one way and then the other as the night shift struggled to make do with less space than usual as Deidre and the officers she'd recruited still occupied their space.

"Jackson, tell me you're having a more productive night."

She turned to see her partner lying on his desk, using his arm as a pillow.

"I guess that's a no."

CHAPTER NINE

Sunrise

DEIDRE RAN HER hands over her face, rubbing sleep—or rather the lack thereof—from her eyes. Lifting her cup, she realized she was, yet again, out of coffee. Grunting, she got out of her chair and made her way into the bullpen, cup hanging by her waist.

"How long ago did someone make this coffee?"

One of the rookie officers looked up at her with bleary eyes. "About twenty minutes."

"Thanks." Stumbling up behind her she found Jackson, cup to his lips. "Morning."

She was met with a grunt as he went back to work.

"I need information on that baby!" She yelled after him and received another grunt in reply.

Grabbing the pot, she poured another cup, doctoring it up with plenty of sugar.

Someday she'd sleep again.

Shaking the thoughts from her head, she went out and looked around the bullpen and saw several officers in various states of exhaustion. Rogers and Hamilton were both slumped over their desks and Deidre had to watch them for a second to make sure they were awake.

But considering they had been on the job for twenty-four hours straight with no sleep, they weren't doing half-bad.

She made her way back to her office. Just as she sat down someone knocked on her door. Looking up, she saw Hamilton standing in the doorway. "Find something?"

"While I was waiting on the last few rosters to come back, I went looking into the girl's recent history, tracking down what they last few days of their lives looked like to see if they overlapped somewhere we're missing. The biggest connection is the rally on Saturday promoting next weekend's soccer tournament."

"What about it?"

"That seems to be the last time the girls were in the same spot. The teams practice at different times, girls lived in different neighborhoods, and went to different churches—"

"Wait." Deidre sat up, coffee temporarily forgotten. "They all went to church?"

Hamilton looked down at his file. "Oddly enough, yes."

Deidre turned to her computer and typed something into Google, taking a look at the number it presented her. "Granted, the odds of people going to church increase with marriage and having children, but it's still something. JACKSON!"

It took a minute but he too was in her office. "What?"

"Oh, so you can talk."

"Ha, ha."

"That theory, the one we were working on yesterday about where the bodies were being laid…"

"What about it?"

"The girls are being laid where kids frequent which, on

that note, we should have someone at schools just in case our unsub gets brave like he did last night."

"Detective?" A rookie stood in the doorway holding a newspaper. "I thought you'd want to see this."

She took the paper and opened it to the front page.

NOTCHER CRASHES MEMORIAL

"Notcher?" Deidre let out a sigh as she read the nickname.

"That's what they're calling him."

"Of course it is. When will people get the memo that giving a killer a nickname gives them power?" Deidre's phone rang, and she flipped it open. "Detective Tordano."

"This is Dispatch. There was a body reported on the beach at Sunray Bay about twenty minutes ago."

"I'm on my way." Deidre hung up and looked at the team assembled in front of her. "We've got another body."

Waves pounded on the deserted beach as Deidre pulled into the parking lot. Hotels lined the bay but if trend held, they would be barely half-full as November set in with its preview of the winter ahead.

Deidre stepped under the tape that had already been rolled out, taking a second to sign in to the log before making her way to where a small crowd of people gathered.

"What do we have?" Deidre walked up to see the body of yet another girl. The analysts once again photographed the notches on her arm.

"Laurie Mull. Age 10. She's only been here a couple hours." Rogers nodded to the body. "Parents just reported her missing about a half-hour ago. Same situation as yesterday with Emily and Jessica."

"Who found the body?"

"A couple of city workers doing cleanup duty. At first they thought she was homeless."

Deidre looked over to see Hamilton standing with a couple of workers, quickly taking down whatever they were saying. Both looked young and the haunted look she could see told her this was the first time they'd ever seen anything like this.

"Is Angus on his way?"

Rogers nodded. "Said something about asking for a raise if we were doing many more mornings like this."

"Him and me both." Deidre knelt down by the beach towel that had covered the girl.

Looking at the arm, she saw two notches. Low number, which Deidre's gut told her wasn't a good thing. A car door snapped her out of her thoughts. Angus approached.

"Morning."

She received a grunt and wondered if there was a trend forming.

"Nice to see you too." She turned back to the body. "Anything on our other victims?"

"Not much more. A lot depends on the lab, and there is only so much I can rush through. What are we on, number six for this guy?"

"Something like that."

Angus nodded to his assistant who brought the gurney over. "Can I take this off your hands?"

"If that means you'll get me something I can use."

She watched as Angus loaded it into a bag before taking it off the beach. People gathered around the outside of the tape, peeking over, as vans and cars flowed toward the beach.

"What is it with serial killers and crowds?" Jackson came up beside her.

"I blame *CSI.*"

—

Deidre pulled into the Starbucks drive-thru and ordered the largest drink she could. Then, cup in the barista's hand, she begged for what would normally be way-too-many shots of expresso. When she finally received the coffee, she took a sip and let out a happy sigh. She turned to head back to the station even though every fiber of her being wanted to head home to her shower and her bed.

She'd barely made it a block when her phone rang. "Tordano."

"It's Rogers."

"What's going on?"

"There's a body at Washington Prep. Teacher found a girl sitting at her desk when she came into her classroom this morning."

"At the teacher's desk or at her own desk?" Deidre turned on her lights and siren and headed towards the school."

"Her own. I'm here now."

"Is she covered?"

"Yeah, with the parachute that they use in gym class."

"I'm on my way." Deidre hung up and called Jackson.

"I just got my coffee."

"Well, drink it on the way to Washington Prep. Victim number seven is there."

CHAPTER TEN

Washington Prep

THE CROWD THAT waited in the parking lot rivaled only the crowd at the vigil as photographers and various onlookers were held there by a team of officers. As Deidre pulled up to the front door in her car, she saw the flash of cameras and knew in her gut that they were pointed right at her.

She dialed Jackson's number. "Zoo is out in full force."

"Joy."

"ETA?"

"Five minutes."

"Alright." She threw the car in park. "I'm going to head in."

"10-4."

Hanging up, she threw her phone in her pocket before turning off her car and stepping out.

"Detective!"

The shouts started right away as press and bystanders both shouted questions at her. Ignoring them, she headed into the front door of the school.

"Let me guess, the security footage is down."

"Unfortunately." Rogers handed her a clipboard. "The camera was turned off and since it was before school hours the log does us no good."

"Witness statement?"

"Already there. Hamilton ran a quick check on the teacher, but she seems to check out. She found our victim when she came in this morning. We cleared the school and checked on the alibis of those present, but they all check out. Most were teachers coming in to start the day; custodial staff say the room hasn't been touched since they completed their rounds yesterday."

"Victim fit our profile?"

"Yeah. Ten year old Ella Donovan."

As he spoke, Deidre walked down the hall skimming over the clipboard. "When was the parachute last seen?"

"Come again?"

"Go find out from the PE teacher when the parachute was last seen. Might tell us how long this plan has been in action or if our unsub is thinking on his feet."

"Yes, Ma'am." Rogers took off down a hallway leaving Deidre to go search for the classroom. Luckily for her, crime scenes have a habit of being obnoxiously noisy.

Crime scene tape covered the doorway and Deidre ducked under it, signed the log, and turned to take in the scene. The desk in the back corner was surrounded by photographers and various officers.

"This is getting old." Deidre spoke up and the officers cleared a path between her and the body. "Have we taken a look?"

"One."

"So, this girl and the one from the beach, umm…" Deidre pulled out her notepad and took a look. "…Laurie

Mull, were our overnight victims. And here I thought we were reaching an endgame."

"I was hoping that was the case." Angus' gruff voice came from the doorway. "I barely got Laurie Mull back to my office before this call came in. Traffic is killer this morning."

"One notch, which means the next girl is probably gone. I can't narrow it down using the teams since I didn't get a chance to check Laurie. But I can add her and Ella in, and I think I know which team is missing."

"Your daughter's team is still in the running?"

"Yes, in fact I think that's where number eight is coming from, because neither of these girls is on her team." Deidre ran her hand over the pocket that held her phone forcing herself to focus on her job and leave keeping an eye on Lilly to Bill.

Letting out a sigh, she turned to the body, looking at the parachute. "No signs of blood. We really need to figure out where the unsub is killing them."

"That still throws me off."

"What, the secondary location? Even after the city is on high alert, this person is able to transport live girls in and corpses out."

Deidre couldn't help but agree with him. "But without knowing where they are being killed, we're still where we were yesterday, only with more bodies."

"Which means it's longer for you to get your results and Sacramento isn't rushing anything else for this case."

"Dead end there. Rogers!"

"Ma'am?"

"Anything else on the knife?"

Rogers shook his head. "But I haven't been back to the

station since most of these businesses opened for the day, so I haven't been able to finish following through."

"Go back and work on that."

Rogers took off, barely missing the gurney as it came into the room. The body was loaded and taken out of the room, leaving a solemn group behind.

"See what you can find."

"I'll do what I can." Angus followed his assistants out.

She turned to see Jackson walk in the classroom. "Sorry. The zoo held me up."

"Jackson, have you found the kid?"

"I'm working on it. But I think I'm almost there." As he said that, his phone rang. "Davidson."

As he talked on the phone, Deidre took a second to look around the room and saw something written on the corner of the board.

MMXIV
XI
V
CVI

"Are those Roman numerals?" She turned to see Jackson frantically making notes as his phone call continued.

"But what do they mean?" Her musings were interrupted by the sound of her phone. "Detective Tordano."

"The Sheppard family just reported their ten-year-old daughter, Audrey, missing."

A feeling grew in the pit of her stomach at the mention of one of Lilly's best friends. This really was coming close to home. "How long ago?"

"They called just a few minutes ago and officers

responded to the call. But they just called and said that you might want to head over there."

"Why?"

"There's something you need to see."

—

As SHE PULLED up to the Sheppard house after hanging up with Jackson, who was heading back to the station to follow up on something from his mysterious phone call, she let out a sigh. The familiar house stood waiting with cars surrounding it, officers walking all along the block and Deidre couldn't help but see all the times Lilly had played on this very street.

Getting out of her car, she nodded to the officer who stood guard at the door. Not saying a word, the officer simply handed her a file.

"Thanks."

Inside, off to her right, she saw Audrey's siblings sitting on the couch, *Frozen* played on the TV as the trio watched. Considering the oldest's complaints about how often the movie was played, that said something about the tone of the house.

A pair of officers stood in the room, watching the kids more than the movie. Both looked up when she paused in the doorway and Deidre simply nodded to them before heading for the kitchen.

In the corner of the kitchen, clutching a coffee cup, sat a distraught Rebecca Sheppard.

"Becca."

"Deidre, is it... did he..."

"I don't know yet, I'm going to go look in just a minute."

"It's her birthday. We were going out tonight. Lilly was

coming over with the team this weekend." The tears began to fall, and Deidre gave her friend a hug.

After a moment, the tears eased and Deidre pulled away. "I need to go see what they found."

Leaving the kitchen, she headed upstairs to Audrey's bedroom and stepped under the tape that lay across it. A group of officers waited in the room and the flash of the camera did nothing to decrease the tension that filled the house.

"What number do we…" Deidre let her sentence trail off as she caught a view of the desk. Sitting on the middle of it was a cupcake with a candle that had burnt into the white icing, charring the sprinkles black.

Beside it, a card sat—one that looked like it was made by a child—that said, "Happy Birthday." A rainbow and smiley face stickers mockingly smiled back at the group.

Beside it, carved into the desk and filled in with the red ink was a number 10.

"I think we're reaching the end game." Her eyes wandered to the collage of photos that sat on a bulletin board above the desk. Photos of friends lined the board and several included her own daughter. Lilly's auburn hair flowed alongside the dark hair of her best friend. Looking at the wall, Deidre was pretty sure she had taken a couple of these.

Seeing her daughter did nothing to ease the feeling in her gut even though she was fairly certain that Audrey was the last victim.

"Sign of a struggle?"

"Just like the other girls. She knew this person."

"Window broken in?"

"Yup."

Deidre rubbed her hands over her face in a mix between

exhaustion and frustration. “Oh, when this is done, I’m sleeping for a week.”

“Got something?”

“Not much of something—or rather several somethings that might become one something.” Deidre nodded to the rest of the officers. “See if there is anything else you can learn from this room, and I’m going to head back to the station.”

“Will do.”

“And I want a full report on my desk in two hours.”

“Yes, ma’am.”

Heading back downstairs, Deidre stopped in the kitchen and found Becca still there. “Where’s Jeff?”

“He’s on his way. He was on a business trip and thought he wouldn’t make it back for Audrey’s birthday.” Becca teared up and Deidre handed her a tissue. “He found out yesterday he would, and his flight lands in an hour.”

“Is there someone to pick him up?”

“I hadn’t thought of that. Ummm, his flight had already taken off before I found out she was missing, so he doesn’t even know.”

“How long has he been gone?”

“A week, before this mess started. Dei, is Audrey going to be okay?”

“I don’t know, Becca.” Deidre took the cup of coffee that was handed to her. “I really don’t know.”

“Oh, Audrey.”

Becca started crying again and Deidre could do nothing more but just be there and attempt to console her friend. “I’m so sorry, Becca.”

The tears continued. “I don’t know how to tell him. He doesn’t know what’s been going on. I haven’t talked about it 'cause I didn't want to worry him and I knew you were on the case."

"I'm doing everything I can." Deidre was starting to feel a broken record.

"I know, I know." Becca blew her nose into a tissue. "It's just my baby. My sweet baby."

"Do… do I need to send someone to pick up Jeff?"

Becca nodded. "Could you?"

"I'll send Bill." Pulling out her phone, Deidre called her husband.

"Everything okay?"

Deidre walked into the hallway out of the earshot of Becca. "The unsub has Audrey."

"No."

"I'm afraid so. But listen, Jeff is due in from his business trip and his flight lands in an hour. He has no idea what's going on and Becca's distraught…"

"What do you need me to do?"

"Can you pick him up? Don't tell him anything just say something came up. Either bring him by the station or get him to call me."

"Sure thing, hon. When's the last time you slept?"

"I think I dozed off for a half hour about four this morning." Deidre made a mental note to make a Starbucks run on the way back to the station. "But I can't sleep, not until I find Audrey and solve this case."

"Does that mean we have to move your birthday dinner?"

"I think we're on the end-game. My gut is saying tomorrow night is still on." Deidre let a small smile fill her face. "Thanks for helping me out."

"Anytime, love."

"I've gotta go say goodbye to Becca and then I need to get back to the station."

"Via Starbucks?"

"You know me so well." Deidre hung up the phone and headed back to the kitchen. "Becca?"

Becca was on the other side of the kitchen watching the kids watch the movie. "Anthony is even watching."

"And he's sick of the movie. Guess that shows how much he wants to keep them happy."

"He always wants to keep his little siblings happy. Big brother."

"Always protecting the little ones." Deidre finished her sentence. "Listen, I've got to get back to the station. The officers upstairs should be about done. If you've got any questions, you have my number."

"Thanks, Deidre."

Deidre nodded as she made her way out of the house. Heading to her car, a jumble of thoughts vied for the bulk of her attention. But at the moment, only one won out.

How many shots of expresso would Starbucks put into one cup of coffee?

CHAPTER ELEVEN

Pieces Coming Together

"Tell me you've got something on that knife."

Rogers hung up the phone and held up a pad of paper. "Most of the processing plants closed or merged. Big names, corporate, minimum wagers won out. That being said, most are on more modern equipment than a knife like that but I think I found the one you're looking for. Sunray Seafood Processing closed their doors six months ago after the economy drove them into bankruptcy."

"Sunray? Like the bay we found Laurie on?"

Rogers looked down at his notes. "Yeah, they do match."

"Keep going."

Straightening his notes, Rogers cleared his throat before continuing. "Most of these plants' previous owners left the area after their businesses closed. Most moved in with families in state, though there was one in Florida."

"What here helps me?"

"Sunray's owners haven't left the area because they have nowhere else to go. The plant closure left them several million in the hole but they are trying to keep the house, though the bank is on the verge of foreclosing. That announcement came a couple days ago."

"The trigger?"

"Perhaps." He handed her the notes. "There's the address."

Glancing at the name, Deidre felt her eyes widen. "She just keeps coming up in this, doesn't she?"

"Who?"

"Alexandra Lestrade, better known as Lexi. Her parents owned Sunray Seafood Processing."

"And the sixth victim was found on Sunray Bay."

Deidre took off for her office. She heard footsteps behind her but didn't stop until she was at the map. Grabbing a blue pin, she stuck it into the beach on the map where Laurie's body was found. Looking at the notes again, Deirdre pulled out a different color pin and stuck that one in less than a mile away.

Jackson stood in the doorway. "What does it mean?"

"It means—we finally have a lead."

"Detective." Hamilton rushed into the doorway tightly gripping a piece of paper. "I found out about the parachute."

"When was it last seen?"

"The fifth. Five days ago."

"Rogers!"

"Ma'am?"

"Call the *Badge City Chronicle*, tell them I need a copy of November fifth's paper."

"Yes, ma'am." He left the office.

"Why do you need the paper?"

Before Deidre could answer, the photographer came in with a couple of folders, holding them out for Deidre. Taking then, she flipped through them until she found the one she wanted. "Here. This was on Ella's classroom's board."

"Roman numerals?" Jackson leaned closer.

"Exactly."

"For those of us who can't read that?" Hamilton looked at the paper.

"If I remember right—and Hamilton just confirmed my hunch—it says, twenty-fourteen, eleven, and five which might mean November fifth, this year."

"What about this?" Jackson pointed at the last line.

"C6. Possible page number?"

"They are. The *Chronicle's* sending a hard copy here. Should be here in about ten minutes." Rogers reappeared at the door.

"What's on C6?"

"The foreclosure notice of the home of the owners of Sunray Seafood Processing." It was a guess, but Deidre's gut was pretty sure. "Hamilton, go check and see on the ownership status of the building. Rogers, go find out if the Lestrades are home."

Both officers took off.

Deidre turned to her partner. "Did you find anyone in Lexi's history that would resort to acts like this?"

"No one sticks out. But maybe that's the point. They've done a good job of hiding."

Deidre caught her map up, sticking pins in the right places. "There's a chance."

"A chance of what?"

"If Lexi's cold case is the heart of this…a vigilante might be using the abandoned warehouse."

"That could be our secondary location."

"It could. But why Lexi, why now?"

"Well, my phone call might explain that." Jackson waved

his cell phone in one hand as he held his notepad in the other. "I found the baby."

"You found her?" Deidre looked up quickly.

"Yup." Jackson popped the "p" with a grin. "Turns out, your hunch is right because Alexandra Lestrade's daughter is none other than, as of today, ten-year-old Audrey Sheppard. Her tenth birthday. Think about it: the day she leaves single digits behind, combined with the fact that the Lestrades are about to lose their home."

"Stressor, trigger, perfect storm for a murder spree."

"By why all eight girls? Why not just Audrey?"

Deidre took a sip of her coffee. "That's the million dollar question, isn't it?"

"Detective?" Rogers stuck his head back in her office. "The Lestrades are home and say they would love to help you in any way they can."

"Good, call them back and tell them we'll be over in a few minutes."

"Yes, ma'am." Rogers disappeared only to be replaced by Hamilton, who held out a newspaper. "Your paper."

"Thanks." Taking it from Rogers, she found the Local Section and then flipped to the sixth page. Sure enough, her hunch was correct: this was the beginning of the public records section and listed the home as going into foreclosure. "And before I have my 'I was right' dance, let's go talk to the Lestrades."

It was after one before Deidre pulled up to the Lestrade house. Bushes that lined the front of the house looked as if they hadn't seen a pair of clippers this year while the already brown grass looked horribly unkempt. Chipping paint showed the fact that the family had paid more attention to keeping the business afloat instead of maintaining their house.

She turned off her car and got out. Letting herself in, the gate behind her squeaked.

She didn't even make it to the front stoop when the door opened and a slightly balding man met her. "Detective Tordano?"

"Yes, Mr. Lestrade?"

"Just George. Would you like to come in?" He stepped aside and waved her into the house, leading. She saw boxes all around, another reminder of what was coming for this family. He had a stoat-like way of movement, that began somewhere in the tilt of his head and thrust of his neck.

"Thank you for agreeing to speak with me, especially under the circumstances."

"Have a seat." A woman came in from what looked to be the kitchen and nodded to the couch.

"Thank you."

"I'm Grace."

"Deidre." Deidre took a seat on the couch as Grace took a seat beside her. George sat in a chair opposite them. "I have a few questions."

"About?"

"Several things actually. First off, I have intel that says that your company might have had access to a knife that looks like this." Deidre pulled out the picture of the suspected murder weapon.

George took the picture, sliding on a pair of reading glasses and looked it over. "It does look like the knives we used for dressing the fish."

"Dressing?"

"Removing the scales and insides from a fish. Back in the

old days, we did it by hand. We still did some the old-fashioned way. The appeal of a smaller business."

"But in the end, people don't care about that." Grace sighed as she crossed her legs. "It's all big business now, how can it be done quickly and efficiently."

"Dear..." George looked over the piece of paper.

"It's just that, that business has been in your family for generations, since not too long after this town was founded over a hundred years ago. And now it's all for nothing. We've lost the business, we're losing this house, and we've lost any chance at ever having grandchildren."

"What?" At this revelation, Deidre pulled out her notebook and began taking notes.

Tears welled up in Grace's eyes. "Lexi can't have kids. Something went wrong when her baby girl was born. She almost bled out, it was awful. The Doctors said she'll never be able to have kids."

"And she couldn't keep the one she had."

"She never got to hold her."

"What?"

"It all happened fast. They took the baby out of the room. They even forced us out so that they could try and figure out the problem," Grace said. "The next thing I know, these men are taking our granddaughter away and we never saw her again. The mayor sealed the records and we were never able to find her. Lexi barely saw her."

"Do you know where Lexi is?"

George let out a sigh. "She usually wanders off, spends today alone. She's never been quite the same since that night. If I could just get my hands..." But his wife patted his arm, and the sentence trailed off.

Deidre tried to wrap her mind around the information she'd just been given. "One last question, if you don't mind."

"What can we help you with?"

"What happened to the factory? Do you know who might have access to the property?"

"It was abandoned. We sold off what we could so it's basically empty. I'm sure anyone who's determined enough could break in."

Shutting her notebook, Deidre stood up. "I think that's all. Thank you so much for your time, I greatly appreciate it. And I'm sorry. About everything."

"Thank you." Grace stood up. "I hope you find the person responsible."

"So do I." Deidre started to leave but stopped. "One more on top of that. What time was the baby born?"

"What was it Grace…about six?"

"6:11PM. She was seven pounds ten ounces and nineteen inches long."

"Thank you for your time." Walking out of the house, she picked up her phone and called the station. "Hamilton, check the records for who owns the former property of Sunray Seafood Processing and get back to me."

Hanging up the phone, Deidre called in dispatch. "I'm issuing a Code 10."

—

"Are you sure?" Deidre pulled into a spot at the courthouse, a partially filled-out search warrant sitting on the seat next to her.

"Positive." Hamilton's voice came through the phone. "The city bought the property about a month after it was abandoned. Plans are in the works to turn the facility into a mini-amusement park to add to the area's tourism. Most of the processing plants are located further down the beach."

"Alright, I'm going to get this warrant signed by the judge and then we're going in."

"I heard you called a Code 10."

"Get Rogers and be ready. You guys deserve to help bring him down."

"10-4, Detective."

Ending the call, Deidre grabbed a clipboard and finished filling out the search warrant. She stopped to make a copy of the finished warrant, then clipped it to the case file. She rushed to the courthouse, making a slow way through security. The security gave her the names of the sitting judges for the day and she made her way to the courtroom of the judge of her choice. Meeting with a bailiff, she said, "I need to speak with Judge Turner as soon as possible."

The bailiff nodded and stepped into the courtroom, shutting the door behind him. Deidre paced back and forth outside the doors until the bailiff stuck his head out. "He wants to know if he needs to clear the room."

"Since this is part of an ongoing investigation I would prefer it—but as usual, I will leave it to his discretion."

The bailiff disappeared and Deidre continued her pacing until she saw several people leaving the courtroom. As the last few people trickled out, she made her way inside to find the honorable Judge Micah Turner sitting on the bench.

"Your honor." Deidre greeted him as she made her way down the center aisle.

Judge Turner peered at her over his rimmed glasses. "Detective, please tell me this is about the case that has had my daughter calling the last few days sick with worry."

"It is, sir." Deidre arrived at the bench and handed him the file.

"You want to search the premises for DNA evidence linking the site to the previous victim, the murder weapon, and possible DNA evidence of the murderer. Why this property?"

"Throughout our investigation we've found several links to a cold case from back in 2004. What notes were made are included in the file for your consideration."

Judge Turner flipped the file open and shook his head. "What evidence do you have that this crime happened?"

"According to the file, a DNA sample was ordered but was never matched to the father. Said sample is still on file, however, and could be matched to Steven Richards. There is also Alexandria Lestrade's statement from both 2004 and one she gave to me yesterday. Both match up."

"Continue."

"All of the victims match the age of the daughter that was born to Lestrade later that year. The bodies were placed in places where someone would take a child, which leads us to think someone is getting revenge for what happened all those years ago."

"Why wait 'til now?"

"We believe the stressor was Sunray Seafood Processing being forced to close its doors six months ago and the trigger was the bank announcing that it was going to foreclose on Alexandria's parents' home five days ago. The first murder occurred a little over 48 hours ago, which also coincides with when news sources started to declare Richards the winner in his race and when our local stations started saying the same."

"Any idea who did this?"

"Not sure. We had originally thought that it was someone close to Lestrade at the time, but one of my officers hasn't found anyone without an alibi. Current consideration is that it was someone who thought they were close to Lestrade and is now trying to get the public attention to right this wrong."

"How are you going to proceed?"

"I've already issued a Code 10 and with your permission, will proceed in with SWAT. Since our unsub is currently holding a victim, it is safe to assume that he might still be there and we need to proceed with caution."

She took a step back as the judge continued to examine the file in front of him. Resisting the urge to pace, tap her foot, or do anything that would give away her current lack of sleep, Deidre waited patiently for his verdict.

"Good luck, Detective." The judge handed her back the file and to her relief, she saw both her form filed as well as his paperwork. "Find this guy."

"Yes, Your Honor."

"And Detective?"

"Yes?" She stopped from where she'd started to go up the aisle.

"The statute of limitations means Richards can't be tried. But that doesn't mean he has to get away with it. But you didn't hear that from me."

"Yes, Your Honor." Deidre smiled as she clutched the file and quickly made her way out of the room.

"Send my courtroom back in, if you don't mind. I'd like to make it home in time for dinner."

"Will do, sir." Deidre stepped back into the hallway and nodded to the bailiff. "The judge would like his courtroom refilled so that he can make it home for dinner."

"Yes, ma'am."

Heading down the hall, Deidre checked the time and saw it was nearing five. Grabbing her firearm on the way out of the courthouse, she turned her phone back on before dialing Dispatch. “I need a Code 11 at 401 Sunray Boulevard ASAP.”

“10-4, Detective.”

Hanging up, Deidre hopped in her car as she dialed Jackson’s number. “I’ve got the warrant, get Hamilton and Rogers and meet me there.”

CHAPTER TWELVE

Sunray Seafood

Siren blaring and lights flashing, Deidre made her way through rush hour traffic towards the beach district. Taking a turn fast enough to make her tires squeal, she caught sight of the front door of the plant and stopped by the two SWAT trucks. The area around the trucks was bustling with SWAT members as Deidre stopped her car just feet away. Getting out, but leaving the lights flashing, Deidre made her way to the trunk as one of the SWAT team commanders made his way over.

"Commander Hadley, nice to see you again." Deidre slid her jacket off and put on a vest.

Commander Hadley rolled a map of the area out onto the hood of her car and she joined him to look over it. "There are only two ways in or out and your uniforms have a hard perimeter established."

"Okay, what's the plan of entry?"

"I'll lead Team 1 into the North Entrance here. Commander Greene will take Team 2 to the South Entrance."

"I'll send my partner with Team B and I'll stay with

Team A. There might be some evidence in that building that will help me nail a conviction."

"Is this about the girls?" Hadley finally looked up from his map.

"Yes."

"What are we looking for?"

"DNA evidence, possible murder weapon." Deidre reached into her car and pulled the knife sketch out. "The coroner thinks it looks a little like this."

Hadley took a photo with his phone and sent it out. "Getting this, team? Possible murder weapon."

"Also, we're looking for blood, possibly lot of it."

"Possibly?"

"I've got a morgue full of girls who supposedly bled out yet no trace of said blood. If this is my secondary location and I think it is, then it might be in here."

Hadley nodded. "Okay. You're with me and Team 1. Your partner is with Team 2."

As he said that, sirens could be heard and Deidre turned to see two cars turn where she had earlier, the screech of their tires rivaling her own. Both cars came to a stop feet from her. Jackson got out of one as Hamilton and Rogers got out of the other.

Ducking into her car, Deidre pulled a quarter out of her cup holder and held it up. "Hamilton, you've been with the department longer so call it."

"Tails."

Flipping the coin, she let it come to rest on the road in front of her before looking at it. George Washington's face looked back at her so she turned to Rogers. "North or South."

"North."

"Alright. That means Rogers is with me and Team A,

Jackson, you've got Hamilton and Team B." She pointed at the locations. We're going to go in from both sides. You guys know what pieces we're missing so you know what to look for. Keep in contact and remember, if this unsub is there..."

"This is it." Jackson finished her thought. "Lexi's baby was born at 6:11 November 10, 2004."

Deidre took in the scene one last time and felt a small smile find its way to her face. "Mac would have a fit if he could see this."

"We look like we're straight out of one of those crime shows."

Looking around, she saw the press had found a gathering spot on the other side of the road blocks that were being set up and a quickly-growing crowd of civilians were lining them as well.

"Still don't get what it is with people and crime scenes." Deidre let out a sigh as she turned back to the task at hand.

"Detective."

This time, both SWAT leaders came up.

"Jackson, you remember Commanders Hadley and Greene."

"Thanks for helping us out tonight." Jackson shook both their hands.

"Detective, if your team is ready, we're ready to give the go order."

Turning to Jackson she nodded. "Ready?"

"Ready when you are."

Turning to Hamilton and Rogers, she got nods before she could even ask the question.

"We're ready, commander."

With one last nod, Jackson, Hamilton, and a team of SWAT members headed around the side of the complex.

It seemed like forever before Jackson's voice came over the radio. "We're in position."

Deidre and her teamed moved into position by the front gate, battering ram at the ready. She took her place next to Officer Hadley as he gave the order. "On my count. 3…2…1…"

—

The team swarmed around Deidre, making their way into various entrances. "With me, Rogers."

Spotting what had been the main entrance, she found the door unlocked and walked on in and was instantly met with a musty smell that told the story of the building's recent past. Flashlight up in one hand, gun by her side in the other, Deidre made her way through the main center hallway, the sound of pounding footsteps through the empty building giving her an idea of where people were.

But she was afraid that it would do the same thing for the unsub.

"Police! Come out with your hands up!" Deidre yelled, her voice echoing down the hallway.

Not surprisingly, she got no response and continued to make her way deeper into the facility, stopping at each and every door to make sure there were no hidden surprises.

This went on as she made her way deeper and deeper until she could hear something.

Hush little baby
Don't say a word
Momma's gonna buy you
A mocking bird

"Rogers, do you hear that?"

She turned to see a nod and grabbed her radio. "This is Tordano and I have ear on a female voice singing."

"10-4, Tordano." Jackson's voice rang out. "What is she singing?"

"Hush little baby."

"The lullaby?"

"Yeah."

And if that mocking bird don't sing
Momma's gonna buy you
A diamond ring

As Deidre continued down the hallway, the singing grew louder. "I think we're near the main packaging room."

And if that diamond ring turns brass
Momma's gonna buy you
A looking glass

"Why a lullaby?" Rogers asked, his tone hushed but still echoing.

"Feeding into the delusion?" Deidre shrugged as they continued down the hallway, turning a corner so that double doors were in sight.

And if that looking glass gets broke
Momma's gonna buy you
A billy goat

Deidre eyed a set of double doors. "This is Tordano. I think I may have something."

"10-4, Deidre."

Deidre paused, pressing her back against the wall by the double doors.

And if that billy goat won't pull
Momma's gonna buy you
A cart and bull

Taking a deep breath, she looked to Rogers before nodding to the doors. "Ready?"

"Let's do this."

And if that cart and bull turn over
Momma's gonna buy you
A dog named Rover

With that, Deidre kicked opened the double door and with gun raised rushed into the room.

"Freeze!"

CHAPTER THIRTEEN

Happy Birthday

DEIDRE HAD TO fight the urge to drop her gun in shock as she took in the sight before her. Sitting on the floor, covered in the ever growing pool of blood, was Lexi Lestrade rocking back and forth. In her arms, she held Audrey and from this angle, Deidre could see the girl was dead. Resting in her hand was a knife. It lay against Audrey's arm, already rich with bleeding notches.

And if that Dog named Rover won't bark
Momma's gonna buy you
A horse and cart

"Alexandria Lestrade, put the knife down."

Deidre slowly walked towards Lexi but it was as if Lexi couldn't hear her.

And if that horse and cart fall down
You'll still be the sweetest baby in town

"Lexi, put the knife down."

"What time is it, Detective?"

Taking a quick glance at her watch, Deidre turned back to Lexi. "6:08."

The knife in Lexi's hand moved, resting point side down on Audrey's arm. "She was born at 6:11. I barely saw her, but when her parents brought her to the rec center a few years ago, I knew, I just knew she was mine. She wasn't supposed to be named Audrey."

"What was she supposed to be named?" Deidre nodded to Rogers who stepped away before she could quietly hear him calling in their location.

"She was supposed to be named Grace—after her grandmother."

"I talked with her earlier. She told me about what happened to you."

"No one listened, no one cared." It was Lexi's turn to check her watch. "6:10. One more minute."

Her hand tighten around the knife. "Lexi, please, she's already gone. I understand that you didn't even get to hold your baby."

"Gone?" She said, frantically, voice rising to a screech. "Gone? No. No one can take her away from me. I lost my daughter and no one cared. No one knew. They didn't know the pain I was feeling. Well, now they know. Now they know what it's like to lose a daughter. They understand my pain. But I'm not going to lose her again. I've lost my daughter for the last time. Now no one can take her."

A quick check to her watch caused a smile to grow on Lexi's face. "6:11"

"This is what it's like to lose a daughter."

With that, she slashed the knife deep into the dead girl's arm.

Lexi continued rocking, but the song changed.

Happy Birthday to you
Happy Birthday to you
Happy Birthday dear Grace
Happy Birthday to you

CHAPTER FOURTEEN

Aftermath

"THE CITY FEELS your pain. Trust me, I have felt your pain for the last few days."

"They don't understand. I lost everything."

Deidre finally reached Lexi and put a hand on her shoulder. "It's over. Lexi. Please, don't make this worse."

The hunched-over figure didn't move, still rocking, still clutching the girl. She'd gone back to humming "Hush Little Baby" as she slipped back into a state where it was as if Deidre wasn't there.

The doors to the room slammed open and Deidre turned to see a group of SWAT members charging into the room.

"Call for the coroner, and the photographer, and the crime scene unit." Deidre knelt down next to Lexi. "Lexi, did you kill the other girls here?"

The humming continued.

"Rogers, help me get Audrey out of her arms so I can get her up."

Rogers knelt down and wrapped a glove around the knife before removing it from Lexi's hand. There wasn't a struggle took the knife, but all that changed after he'd sat and tried to remove Audrey.

"No! She's mine! Don't touch her!"

Deidre grabbed a hand as it went to swat Rogers away and put it behind Lexi's back. The other hand soon followed as Deidre cuffed her behind her back. "Alexandria Lestrade, you are under arrest."

Pulling her so she was standing up, Deidre led her outside as Rogers sat the body down.

"Rogers, check the scene. See if there's any evidence of the other murders." Deidre led Lexi out of the room and down the hall. "Jackson, do you copy?"

"Loud and clear."

"I have a suspect in custody and am proceeding out of the building."

"10-4."

They walked in silence as they made their way down the hallway. As it was, there were two eye witnesses to one murder, and, depending on what Rogers found, they might be able to link her to more.

It was dark by the time they reached the front door. Deidre led Lexi out and ignored the flash of cameras that met them as they stepped outside. Lexi's head hung as they made their way to one of the cars. Guiding her head with her hand, Deidre got her settled into the back of the car.

"Watch her." She turned to one of the officers who was keeping an eye on the barricades.

"Yes, ma'am."

Deidre turned back to the building. An idea hit her, and she pulled out her phone and quickly dialed a number. "Carly, it's Deidre."

"Detective Tordano! Are you going to give me a quote on what's going on down at that warehouse?"

"Not quite. Remember how I told you that I owed you after you helped me with the Kipriyanov case a few months back?"

"Well, that quote would be a start."

"I've got something better." Deidre walked back into the building. "Hope you got your pad ready?"

"Is this on the record?"

"Yes and no. I don't want my name mentioned, but I can point you in the right direction."

"I'll take it—what do you have?"

"What do you know about Steven Richards?"

"The politician? California's future governor and the golden boy of the state?"

Deidre felt a very real smile grow on her face. "Not such a golden boy."

—

THE STATION WAS a lot quieter as the night shift settled back into its normal routine.

But Deidre's office was still in a state of chaos with boxes ready to pack up the contents of the boards—to keep them safe until Lexi would be put on trial. For the last few minutes Deidre had alternated between packing up the case, filling out the report, and chugging yet another cup of coffee.

"How many is that for you?"

She looked up to see her father standing in the doorway of her office.

"I lost track about three this morning."

"When did you last sleep?"

"What time is it?"

"About nine."

"Is it that late already? Wow, time flies when you're wrapping up a case."

"So you got your man?"

"Woman."

Surprise filled her father's face. "Woman?"

"It was Lexi, Dad."

"Alexandria Lestrade?"

Deidre nodded as she sat down, writing up the rest of the events of the evening to be added to the stack of reports on the other victims. "She wanted the city to feel her pain and we will. Eight girls with the whole world ahead of them and like that..." She snapped her fingers. "They're gone."

"You can't beat yourself up." Her dad pulled up a chair and took a seat, picking up the report she had left on her desk and took the photos of Grace, Natalie, Emily, Laurie, Ella, Audrey, Jessie, and Katelyn and put them into the box. Eight smiling girls and then a picture of...

"I hate cases like this," he continued. "Someone wronged so hard that they let it fester, brewing blind in their gut until they lash out with whatever's at hand. Sometimes booze, sometimes drugs—here, little girls." He turned away. "I hate cases like this. It makes me wonder if dad was right. That by the book doesn't do anything but kill more people. You know...Deidre. I think he would've done something to Richards. Years ago. At the start. But we did it by the book. That's something. We can't beat ourselves up for following the rules. It holds the world together."

"It's hard not to. For the last few days, I've had to try and figure this mess out and there was nothing. I felt like every time the phone rang it would be someone saying Lilly has been found somewhere and the idea that something happening to her." She continued to pack the room up in silence until the once-crowded boards were emptied into the boxes. "Besides, I should have known better."

"Known what?"

"Known not to automatically discount Lexi. I had her in here, Dad. And I just saw her as a victim."

"The fact that you thought it was a man isn't surprising. Do you know the odds of this being caused by a woman? Plus…it's Lexi. God. I did it, didn't I? It's all coming back to get me."

"I wouldn't say that. You're a good—"

"*You're* a good cop, Deidre. And I'm proud of how far you've come. Don't dare say that about me." Silence held them tight until he added, "Please go home, Deidre. I'll just sit here."

"I'm going, I'm going." Deidre threw up her hands. "I'm not a kid anymore."

"No, you're not."

"Oh, and Dad?"

"Yeah?"

"You might want to pick up tomorrow's paper. Something tells me it's going to be good."

—

BADGE CITY CHRONICLE

Friday, November 11, 2014

POLICE ARREST SUSPECT
IN NOTCHES TRIAL

By: Isaiah Walsh

Last night, the Police Department arrested a

suspect in connection to the string of murders that have been happening since Saturday.

Alexandria Lestrade, 29, was arrested on eight counts of murder and several counts of trespassing at what had formerly been her parents' seafood processing plant.

Lestrade allegedly murdered eight girls from the Westlake Rec Center, beginning with 10-year-old Grace Miller on Tuesday. Funeral arrangements for the victims had yet to be made at press time, but will be available on our website.

The head detective on the case, Deidre Tordano, was unavailable for comment.

Lestrade grew up here in the city, raised by owners of Sunray Seafood Processing which closed down earlier this year. She went to the local community college where she earned a double major in Business Administration and Sports Management before taking over the Westlake Rec Center in 2009.

Her parents, Grace and George Lestrade, were also unavailable for comment at press time. They owned Sunray Seafood Plant, the disastrous closure of which occurred last year.

Lestrade is unmarried and has no children.

Her arraignment is scheduled for noon today.

—

BADGE CITY CHRONICLE

Tuesday, November 11, 2014

VICTIMS REMEMBERED

The city mourns the loss of eight girls who were taken from us through acts of senseless violence. The *Badge City Chronicle* would like to take the chance to remember the lives of these young girls.

1. Grace Miller

Grace Miller was the daughter of Jason and Stephanie Miller. She was also the proud sister of Leslie (12), Harry (7) and Lilly (5). She was in Mrs. King's fourth grade class at Lighthouse Elementary School. Grace loved to spend her free time playing soccer at Westlake Rec Center where she played for the Red Wings, playing with her American Girl dolls, reading and writing short stories in her journals. She hoped to someday become a writer and help little girls like her learn to write and play soccer.

2. Jessie Phillips

Jessie Phillips was the daughter of Jason and Sophie Phillips. She was the oldest sibling with a younger brother, Oliver (7) and a sister Chloe (4). She was in fourth grade in Mrs. Harvey's class at Westlake Elementary. Jessie could be found using most of her free time playing soccer at Westlake Rec Center where she played for the Green Goals. She enjoyed playing the piano and riding her bike. She had hoped to one day become a veterinarian.

3. Emily Lee

Emily Lee was the daughter of Matthew and Heather Lee and the youngest of three siblings with two sisters, Amelia (16) and Michelle (12) Emily enjoyed spending time with her family. She was in Ms. Wright's fourth grade class at Lakeview Christian School. Her hobbies included playing soccer at Westlake Rec Center where she played for the Maroon Mavericks, reading, and participating in Christian Kids Theater. She hoped to one day become an actress.

4. Katelyn Summers

Katelyn Summers was the daughter of David and Angela Summers and had one brother Kevin (5). She was in Mr. Hopkins' fourth grade class at Jefferson Street Elementary. Her free time was split between playing soccer for the Yellow Rays at Westlake Rec Center, playing the trumpet, and singing. She had hoped to one day become a singer and go on American Idol.

5. Natalie Parks

Natalie Parks was the daughter of Brian and Melissa Parks and was one of three siblings with a brother, Daniel (16) and a sister Joy (7). She was in fourth grade with Mrs. Edwards at Grace Christian School. She played soccer at Westlake Rec Center and was a forward for the Blue Lagoons, read anything she could get her hands on, and enjoyed photography. She wanted to someday travel the world taking photos.

6. Laurie Mull

Laurie Mull was the daughter of Mark and Jennifer Mull and was one of five siblings with two brothers Chris (13) and Will (2) and two sisters Amy (7) and Lexi (4). Laurie was in fourth grade and in Mr. Reid's class at Franklin Street Elementary school. She loved playing soccer for the Silver Linings and spent the rest of her free time reading, riding her bike, and playing with her Barbies. She hoped to someday be a teacher.

7. Ella Donovan

Ella Donovan was the daughter of Jack and Ruby Donovan and is also survived by a younger brother, Tommy (4). She was in Mrs. Knight's fourth grade class at Kemper Street School. She was the goalie for the White Warriors at Westlake Rec Center and when not playing soccer she was usually playing with her American Girl dolls or playing her guitar. Ella had hoped to one day become a social worker and help kids who were less fortunate.

8. Audrey Sheppard

Audrey was the daughter of Anthony and Rebecca Sheppard and had three siblings, Brian (13), Nicole (9), and Hannah (5). She was in fourth grade at 5th Street Elementary and in Mr. Robinson's class. She played soccer for the Gold Stars at the Westlake Rec Center. Her free time was spent reading and working with puzzles. She had hoped to be a scientist one day and cure Brian's diabetes.

The *Badge City Chronicle* would like to offer its deepest condolences to the families of the victims.

—

BADGE CITY CHRONICLE

Wednesday November 12, 2014

LOCAL GOLDEN BOY HAS DARK PAST

By: Carly Richards

After being elected to office in Sacramento just last week, Steven Richards, son of former mayor Helene Richards, has been called the city's "Golden Boy." He has also made his way onto the short list for future governor of California.

Recent events have raised the question as to whether this golden boy's reputation is as golden as was once thought. An unnamed source shared with the Chronicle some details that have since been verified and tell a different tale.

The date was February 14, 2004 and Richards was a high school senior who took Alexandria Lestrade out to dinner. Yes, the same Lestrade who was arrested Monday on eight counts of murder. According to police records, Lestrade came in to the station late that night to report that Richards raped her. A DNA sample was taken but never processed as Lestrade later dropped the charges.

Thanks to recent statements, it has been revealed that former mayor Richards bribed the Lestrade family in an attempt to keep them from pursuing the case. Nine months later, Lestrade gave birth to a baby girl. The child was taken into protective custody and placed up for adoption.

When asked about the truth of these events, Richards (mother and son) refused to comment. Steven declined to provide a DNA sample, which could clear his name once and for all.

Unfortunately, due to the Statue of Limitations, Richards can no longer be formerly charged.

CHAPTER FIFTEEN

A Time for Everything

"You made it." Lilly looked up and smiled, but Deidre noticed it didn't quite reach her eyes. Instead, they showed evidence of all the tears that had been shed the last few days.

"I told you I would." Deidre took a seat beside Lilly. Bill put his arm over her shoulder. "Thanks for bringing her, hun."

Before Bill could answer, the music rose in volume and the assembly stood. Deidre watched as Audrey's family made their way to the pews at the front of the church. Becca's eyes met hers as she passed by and Deidre could see the heartbreak there.

The family took their seats before the rest of the room and they all watched as the coffin was closed for the last time. Finally, Alan Jacobs took the stage and looked out over the room. "Thank you for coming today to celebrate the life of Audrey Faith Sheppard. To begin, family friend, Deidre Tordano will read from Ecclesiastes three."

Deidre rose from her pew and made her way to the stand that had been left on the stage. She still wasn't sure why she had agreed to read, partially out of guilt that she hadn't worked fast enough to prevent this, she supposed, and partially for Lilly. Otherwise, she hated speaking in front of people,

Reaching the podium, she grabbed hold of the mic and pulled the page out of her pocket. "I'm reading from the New Living Translation."

Taking a deep breath, she began though her thoughts couldn't help but swim.

"For everything there is a season, a time for every activity under heaven. A time to be born and a time to die. A time to plant and a time to harvest."

Sure there was a time to die, but as Deidre glanced at Jeff and Becca, she couldn't help but wonder why it was that that time came so soon. No parent should have to go through what they were going through.

"A time to kill and a time to heal. A time to tear down and a time to build up." She almost scoffed as she read those words. It was almost ironic that that line was in this portion of scripture. If Becca hadn't insisted, Deidre would have picked something else to read. But the Bible didn't mean to kill like this: leaving a large portion of a city devastated and unsure of why.

She thought of Lexi. By this time, she would be sitting in a cell, awaiting trial since she wasn't granted bail. There was already talk of the DA going for the death penalty.

"A time to cry and a time to laugh. A time to grieve and a time to dance." Though this verse did give her hope, that maybe someday Lilly would once again laugh and dance around to that pop music she seemed to love so much. But right now was a time to cry and grieve. All over the city, people were doing just that.

"A time to scatter stones and a time to gather stones. A time to embrace and a time to turn away." Deidre desperately hoped that families would embrace each other and not turn away from these tragedies.

"A time to search and a time to quit searching. A time to keep and a time to throw away." She searched, searched for that answer until she found it. She just wished she hadn't been that late.

"A time to tear and a time to mend. A time to be quiet and a time to speak." What had made Lexi decide it was now the time to speak? Why now? Why this way? If her father had done something years ago, if he hadn't stayed silent, would Audrey still be alive? Were their deaths on his head?

"A time to love and a time to hate. A time for war and a time for peace. What do people really get for all their hard work? I have seen the burden God has placed on us all. Yet God has made everything beautiful for its own time. He has planted eternity in the human heart, but even so, people cannot see the whole scope of God's work from beginning to end. So I concluded there is nothing better than to be happy and enjoy ourselves as long as we can. And people should eat and drink and enjoy the fruits of their labor, for these are gifts from God."

Nodding to Becca and Jeff, she folded the piece of paper and made her way back to her seat. Bill's arm slid back over her shoulder and she took his hand again before letting out a deep breath. A hand landed on her lap and she found her daughter looking at her; Deidre took her hand in her free one.

The service passed, songs were sung and the obituary

was read, then the floor was opened up for people to share a memory of Audrey.

Lilly slid off the pew and went past Deidre, something balled up beneath her arm. She disappeared at the side of the stage and came up wearing her jersey over her dress. The mic was lowered for her and she looked out at the crowd before her eyes met Deidre's.

Oh, she was so nervous, and Deidre nodded, giving her what she hoped was a reassuring smile.

Lilly nodded and looked down at the casket. "I met Audrey when we were in preschool. We both brought dolls to class the first day and later we all had a tea party together. The next year, when we were old enough for the little league, I wasn't sure if I wanted to do it, but she convinced me that we should and for the last few years we've had a blast."

Tears welled up in Lilly's eyes and she paused for a moment. "The tournament might not happen, but I think Audrey and the other girls would want us to play. I might not have known them that well, but I did know Audrey and she's going to be cheering us on."

Lilly looked back down at the casket. "Mommy says you're in Heaven now, Audrey. You're getting to have tea parties with Jesus and see your Grandma again. But I'm going to miss you here."

With that, Lilly left the stage but paused at the casket, reaching her hand up, but she couldn't quite reach the top to put something there. Before Deidre could get up, Jeff was there and gave her a boost. When Lilly moved away, Deidre could see the gold star that now rested on the top of the coffin.

Tears pouring down her face, Lilly returned to her seat

next to Deidre. With a sigh, Deidre put her arm around her daughter and pulled her close and let her cry.

—

The Indian summer that they'd been enjoying made a slight comeback the next week as the tournament went on as scheduled. The makeshift memorial had morphed into something a little more permanent, with plans to create an official one and dedicate it at the beginning of next year's season.

Deidre parked her car in the lot before stepping out and draping her jacket on her arm. The Rec Center was bustling with activity as the teams were making their way out to the nearby fields. Leaves crunched under her feet as she made her way to the stands.

Looking up, she found Bill sitting, trying to keep Carrie and Colton from accidentally falling off the bleachers. Mac was sitting below them, reading over a script.

"Mommy!" Carrie was the first to spot her.

"Hey hun.," Bill called out as Deidre made her way up the stairs to them.

Sitting on the other side were Becca and Jeff, who had come to every game the Gold Stars had played out of support. Audrey's jersey was draped on the bench as her teammates came to place water bottles in their spots before making their way to the field for warm-ups.

It had been a good tournament, even by 10-year-old little girl soccer standards. All eight teams had brought out their best in order to pay respect to their fallen teammates, but in the end, only the Gold Stars and the Red Wings had made it to the championship game.

The stands were quickly filling up as members of the

other six teams, parents, friends, and— thanks to the case—a curious public came to watch the big game.

"Glad I made it." Deidre sat down on the bench beside her husband and promptly had Carrie curl up in her lap. Kissing the top of her head, Deidre gave her little girl a hug. "Were you a good girl?"

Wide eyes met her and she received a nod.

"Is that a script, Mac?"

"Yeah." Her oldest smiled back at her.

"Did you get a part?"

"It's just a couple of lines."

"That's great!" Deidre smiled.

Leaning over her husband, she smiled at Becca and Jeff. "Glad you guys could make it."

"We wouldn't miss this. Audrey would have been ecstatic to be in the championship game." Becca's eyes filled with tears.

"Win or lose, they'll do her proud." Deidre smiled before leaning back over to catch sight of her mom and dad making their way up. "Over here, guys!"

They made their way up and sat beside Mac as Colton made his way to his grandfather's lap. After the week she'd had, Deidre couldn't help but smile at the sight of her family together, safe, sound, and whole. Though her heart still broke for her friends a few feet away who weren't so lucky.

A whistle blew down on the field and Deidre turned to see the teams gathering at center field. A few left to take a seat on the bench as the rest took their places, including Lilly in the goal.

"Go, Lilly!" Deidre called out.

"Yeah, Lilly!" Colton and Carrie cried in unison.

She looked over and they all waved and Deidre could

see the smile that filled her face. It lasted until the whistle blew and she turned back to focus on the ball.

Both teams played great and when they took a few minutes at half time, neither team had scored. The stands were packed and people lined the fields by that point and Carrie was sound asleep in Deidre's arms. She rubbed her hand slowly up and down her daughter's back.

"Good game so far." Her dad turned to face her and she could see Colton asleep in his arms.

"It is. Surprised these two fell asleep."

"They were bouncing off the walls earlier, I couldn't get them to take a nap." Bill shrugged. "I tried to warn them."

Deidre shook her head. "Well it would either be this or they would be bored by now. This way, they can say they were here."

She looked down on the field to see Lilly drinking from her water bottle, sweat glistening on her forehead. But even though she looked tired, there was a determination in her eyes that Deidre knew was from Audrey's absence.

The squeal of a megaphone drove Deidre from her thoughts and she saw a man stand at centerfield.

"Thank you all for coming out to the last game of this season. This community was hit last week by a tragedy, but these girls rose above it and played their hearts out. Also, thanks to your donations, we have raised a lot of to make sure that rape victims in our area will have their voices heard."

Unlike Lexi's.

Even with the passing thought, Deidre smiled at that comment, proud of the families who had come together and made the decision to see if they could help stop something like this from happening again.

"Also, we heard that Detective Deidre Tordano is present

today. Her little girl, Lilly, is doing a great job as the Gold Star's goalie. Deidre Tordano, please, stand up."

Applause started and Deidre shook her head, letting out a groan. Finally she stood and felt her cheeks blush as she hurried to sit back down.

"Please send our thanks to your fellow co-workers for all they did. Now, please join me in a moment of silence as we remember those who were lost.

It was surprising just how quiet that many people could get but after a minute, the man lifted the megaphone back to his mouth. "And with that, let's finish out this tournament."

Cheers rang out as the teams took the field and as play resumed, Deidre settled in to watch it with her family.

—

M.H. Norris is a genre nomad, wandering freely between crime, science fiction, fantasy, and spy-fi. She's an executive producer and writer for *Time Walkers*, an interactive webseries (from Flamero Interactive), and a staff writer for 18th Wall Productions' Alice in Wonderland-inspired audio drama series, code-named *Mira Harbor.*

Made in the USA
Lexington, KY
28 March 2015